ALBANY

PART ONE

THE HOME

OF HER DREAMS

Nigel Heath

ISBN: 9798362160173

My grateful thanks in the preparation of Albany House are due to Marc Bessant Design, my wife, Jenny Davis, Mary Watts and Alexandra Bridger for literary support, to artist Maureen Langford for the cover picture and to my walking companion and poet, Peter Gibbs, for his technical support. Peter's poetry anthology, Let The Good Rhymes Roll, is also published on Amazon.

Chapter 1

Laura Jameson couldn't resist peering into the estate agency window every time she walked home after dropping Lottie and Luke, aged eight and ten, off at the village school. Yes, the house of her dreams was still there and had not yet been defaced by one of those nasty red 'under offer' stickers. The Jameson family lived in Cherry Grove, a small development of new homes, several of which were thatched, while others had half-timbered features, because it was the builder's boast that he built in the local style, but the result was they all looked rather twee and were quite small inside.

Laura and her husband, Ben, were newlyweds when they moved in, but now, they needed more space and she'd spotted Albany House, a former rectory, three miles away in the small wooded village of Little Oreford and had instantly fallen in love with it.

Unlike most such period properties, it was not an overly large and rambling early Victorian pile, but of a more reasonable size and neatly proportioned with a central front door and large windows. It reminded her of the picture on the cover of one of her favourite childhood story books and this was probably why she now coveted

4

it. Albany House was on the market for £485,000, which she knew was more than just a little outside their financial comfort zone, no matter which way she mentally rearranged their domestic budget in the small hours while Ben slumbered. She had not yet plucked up the courage to raise the subject because she knew he would dismiss the idea out of hand and that would be the end of her daydream.

I should really think myself lucky,' she told herself. Hampton Green is a friendly place; we have great neighbours here and the kids can walk to school. If we lived in Little Oreford, I'd have to drive them there and back every morning.

Anyway, enough of all that, because they had people coming around for supper and that meant popping over to the Allway Centre superstore and designer outlet complex on the outskirts of Draymarket, the only place nowadays, she could buy fresh fish. It was an eight mile round-trip from Hampton Green, but Little Oreford would be much closer if they were ever able to buy Albany House, Laura mused as she drove home with the fish. Besides that, there was also a lovely walk from the village across the fields to the child friendly Black Swan in the village of Yardley Upton. So that would make a lovely round-trip on a weekend.

While Laura and Ben were a sociable couple and fully engaged with community life through the school, St Mary's Church and the village hall, they were not really dinner party people, but had somehow been drawn into playing hosts that evening. Months earlier, they'd accepted a surprise supper invitation from a couple, who were more acquaintances than friends, and arrived to find there were four other couples already seated in the spacious lounge.

Everyone got on well, so it was no surprise when they received second and third invitations as their fellow guests reciprocated in turn. "The trouble is that we should never have accepted the second invitation from John and Lynn Squires, because I didn't really take to them and then we'd have been out of the loop," grumbled Ben as he and Laura faced up to the fact that it was now their turn to do the entertaining and there was really no way out of it. "It's not really that I mind entertaining if it's for our own close friends, but the trouble is that the Squires and all the others are not really our friends, they're all more affluent than us for a start and are always going on about their expensive holidays and their social life at the golf club."

He and Laura were sitting together at the kitchen table discussing their forthcoming party after the kids were in bed. "It's OK for me because I'll just be taking everyone's coats, making polite conversation and serving the drinks, while it's you who will be under all the pressure," he said. "We could always order takeaways," she suggested and at that they began laughing at the thought of the look on the Squires' and their other guests' faces when they were asked if they wanted an Indian, Chinese or fish and chips. "Look we'll have a cold starter, say some smoked salmon with avocado, and I'll do your favourite fish and vegetable dish, which is all cooked in one pot, so, once that's prepared, and in the oven, there won't be that much to do other than some broccoli spears to go on the side and I'll make a tart for dessert."

Laura spent most of the day of the dinner party preparing the meal. The children were being picked up from school by her friend, Sarah, and taken back to hers for a sleepover with her twins, Oliver and Andrew, who were in the same years as Lottie and Luke and were all great friends. Ben made a big effort and got home early from Brooks Hospital, just outside Draymarket, where he was an extremely hard-pressed Senior Administrator in an organisation already creaking at the knees. Everyone arrived on time bearing flowers, wine and chocolates and were on good form and appreciative, so much so, that Laura began asking herself what she and Ben had made all the fuss about.

She was preparing to bring the dessert in from the kitchen, while half listening to the conversation percolating through from their small dining room, when someone mentioned 'Albany House' and suddenly, she was on full alert. She entered the room, apricot tart expertly balanced on the palm of one hand and cream jug in the other because she hadn't been a waitress in her student days for nothing. However, the perplexed look on her face was noticed instantly by Ben, who shot her a puzzled glance. Lynne Squires, who'd been in mid flow, switched conversations to compliment their host on the sweet. "I'm a bit of a dab hand when it comes to apricot tarts because they're one of the kids' favourites and that's not forgetting Ben," she said, smiling as she sat down and started cutting it into slices. "So, what was that you were saying about Albany House over at Little Oreford?" another of their guests obligingly asked. "Now. Where was I?" said Lynne. "Oh yes. John and I have

8

booked a viewing. The place has been on the market for months. I know it's a bit out of the way, but it's got charm and a good size garden and with a little doing up, it would make a perfect holiday let investment." Now her husband, a banker who went up to town on Monday's and returned on Thursday's, was saying that no matter what happened, property was always a safe investment, but Laura hardly heard him because her heart had started thumping. 'That's my house you wealthy stuck-up bastards. It isn't fair. It bloody well isn't fair!' she fumed. "Are you all right, darling?" Ben asked, seeing her face had flushed, always a tell-tale sign she was becoming agitated. "No. I'm suddenly not feeling very well. I think maybe I should go and lie down for a few minutes." The truth was that she suddenly couldn't bear to spend another moment in that pompous couple's company.

Laura got slowly to her feet, as did John and several of their guests, all expressing concern. She went into the lounge, lay down on the couch, now sagging in the middle from overuse, and listened through closed eyes as Ben took over serving the tart and made small talk for a while, until everyone agreed that perhaps it would be best if they all went home. He rounded up coats and their guests said their goodbyes while hoping Laura was going to be all right. "Are you feeling any better? You didn't look yourself when you came in with the tart," he asked, after closing the door on the Squire's, who were always the last to leave. "I'll be all right in a minute," she smiled weakly. "I know you didn't want them to chat on and on, but suddenly feeling ill was a bit extreme." She smiled again and there was a pause as Ben chose his words carefully.

"Look, we've been together long enough for me to recognise the signs when something's really upset you, so what was it?" His voice was full of gentle concern. Maybe this was the moment to tell him about her dream. If she didn't, she just knew he would go on worrying, because Ben was a worrier and if she chose to keep her secret, just how was she going to cope with seeing the Squires get their grabbing hands on her house? Laura let out a long sigh, reached out and took Ben's hand. "I've had a pipedream for months about Albany House in Little Oreford being our family home for the rest of our lives, because it would be so perfect for that."

Now she was beginning to feel guilty about keeping all this from him. "But I didn't tell you because you're under so much pressure at work and I knew in my heart of hearts we simply couldn't afford it anyway." She bit her lip. "I know I should have just put the whole stupid idea out of my mind and been thankful for what we have, but somehow, I just couldn't stop myself looking in Randall's property display window every time I walked past to see if it had been sold and I guess that just kept on keeping the dream alive. Then when I heard the house mentioned while I was in the kitchen just now and Lynne casually let it out that they were going to view it as a possible holiday home investment just because they are loaded and could, it was all too much for me." There were tears in her nut-brown eyes and a dampness as just a few trickled down her elfin-like face with her short, almost cropped black hair.

It was that face which had instantly attracted Ben to this fellow university student, who he literally bumped into at a Fresher's Fair as they both leaned forward to pick up a leaflet.

"I do wish you'd told me rather than keeping all this bottled up inside." They sat together in silence. Ben leaned forward and kissed the softness at the back of her neck and then had an idea, which came to him out of nowhere. "Perhaps John and Lynne are about to make your dream come true after all. You're right; we could never have afforded Albany House, but it seems pretty clear they can and if they do buy the place, they could rent it to us. "We could let ours out to cover the mortgage and probably for more than we'd have to pay the Squire's and actually be better off." Laura scrambled to come to terms with the suggestion and her immediate reaction was one of indignation. While she really wanted Albany House, how could she bear the fact that even if they rented it and made it their home, she would always know it was not theirs and that John and Lynne could give them notice and take it back just whenever it suited them. Besides that, there would be no point in making any improvements because, in the end, it would only be benefitting the Squire's. She began shaking her head, voicing her objections as she did so, but Ben was surprised to find himself warming to the prospect. He'd actually started finding their neat little home a little claustrophobic and the thought of having space where the kids could have a real garden in which to romp and play, instead of the neat little plot, where they were always being told to stop kicking their balls into the flowerbeds, was beginning to appeal to him.

His life at work was becoming ever more manic with constant bed shortages and all the other problems of running an extremely busy hospital with the rising pressures on space and resources. Then to come home to what was little more than a comfortable shoebox in a small cul-de-sac with open plan front gardens, was not exactly the balm that soothed his nerves. "OK, rather than dismissing the idea out of hand just because we're not in a position to buy it at the moment, why don't we book a viewing?" Whether he consciously put just a little more emphasis on the phrase 'at the moment' he didn't know, but Laura picked up on it immediately and could feel her spirits lifting. "There wouldn't be any harm in just looking," she agreed. "I'll pop in tomorrow morning and see if I can get a viewing for some time on Saturday, when we can all go. Maybe we shouldn't tell anybody about it, otherwise it'll be all around the village and John and Lynne would be bound to find out."

Chapter 2

Royston Randall, sole proprietor of Randall's estate agents in the High Street, always wore a three-piece suit. He had four of them in his wardrobe and decided each morning which he should wear in relation to just how he was feeling. Weekends were his busiest times when he was at his most optimistic and so he donned his smart light cream suit and added a dark brown handkerchief to his breast pocket by way of a nice contrast. Royston was nudging forty, but his slim waistline never varied and, therefore, by wearing his suits in rotation he was making them last a very long time. This would never be noticed by his clients, but his two get-up-and-go sales assistants, Heather and Hannah, who were an item and had been with him for nearly three years, certainly did. They would bet over their breakfast coffee each morning whether it was to be a cream, dark blue, light grey or dark brown suit day. They'd occasionally talked of finding other jobs, but Royston was a generous and kind hearted employer whose Christmas bonus shared between them was always almost half the firm's annual profit and this festive bounty financed their three weeks over Christmas and

New Year break, when they jetted off to exotic locations around the world. They were, in truth, his unofficial partners and the harder they worked then the more they actually earned if the business prospered. Royston, being a shrewd man, had calculated years before that if he really looked after his assistants, then it would reduce the chances of their setting up in opposition to him in an area where he had remained unchallenged.

He was in a particularly good mood that early spring morning because the weather was set fair, which would bring out the home hunters, and he'd had two requests for viewings of Albany House, which had been a 'sticker' in his window for some months. Royston disliked 'stickers,' because they tended to suggest he was falling down on his job. The property had belonged to the last full-time rector of St Michael's, Little Oreford, whose widow had clung on there for many years after his death before finally going to join him in the now overgrown churchyard. Albany House had been inherited by a nephew from the North of England, who paid one visit and had shown little interest in the property, which, following years of neglect, was in a pretty rundown state. Royston suggested a realistic selling price of £325,000, bearing in mind the considerable sum required to bring the house back from internal near dereliction, but the nephew was not impressed. He knew something about property and as the roof appeared to be sound, he would put Albany House on the market for £485,000 and was happy to sit back and wait until a buyer came along. Royston accepted the nephew's instructions with a smile, but was inwardly fuming as the prospect of an early sale and a quick profit was squashed. Clients of inherited property, who could not wait to get their hands on the cash, were the norm and were to be encouraged. Clients like Anthony Allen, the new owner of Albany House, who were simply not in any rush to claim their bounty, were a pain in the bum.

Several people went to look around the property in the weeks after it went on the market, but when they saw that most of the ground floor rooms had damp patches on external walls and that the sills of the single-glazed windows mostly had rot in them, they faltered. Then when they realised the property would need re-wiring and a new central heating system, they walked away, having made realistic offers, which Anthony Allen rejected out of hand. Today, however, might just be different, Royston mused as he drove to work in his mid-range estate car that had enough room in the back to carry his sign boards. He had a far more expensive soft top sports car at home in the garage, which only came out when he wasn't working, because the last thing, he wanted was for people to think him a wealthy man living on fat commissions at their expense. Yes, today just might be different, because he knew the Squires were well heeled and had already indicated their interest in Albany House as a long-term investment. Having sold them their large property on the exclusive Old Barn development, he'd pretty quickly realised this couple were not short of a bob or two. Royston was not so sure that the couple viewing in the afternoon were in any way serious contenders. He'd often seen Mrs Jameson looking in his window and when she'd booked the viewing and had given him her address, he realised instantly there was no way that anyone selling in Cherry Grove would make enough of a capital gain to be able to afford Albany House. Still, they might have been left some cash, he reasoned hopefully.

The satisfying aroma of freshly brewing coffee filled his nostrils as he entered the office. Heather was already on the phone fixing an appointment, so Hannah got up from her desk and disappeared into their small kitchen to fix him a brew. Both women, now in their early forties, were slim and wore designer glasses, but that was as far as the resemblance went, because their taste in clothes was completely different. Heather, who had short cropped blonde hair and fine features, was quite reserved in her choice of styles, while Hannah, whose rounder face was more open, had shoulder-length dark hair and dressed far more flamboyantly. Just occasionally she pushed the boundaries to see how far she could go before Royston put his foot down.

The two women had met while working in a busy South London library, but eventually found their way to Hampton Green during a touring holiday and had lunch in The Red Lion. They could never resist looking in estate agency windows and on Post Office notice boards and were quick to spot there was an attractive barn to let in a rural setting next to the parish church. The rental looked incredibly reasonable by shoe box flat in South London standards and they began fantasising about escaping to the country. Two doors down, they came to Randall's and immediately spotted a second notice reading 'Staff Required, Apply Within.' Before they knew it, they'd entered the large office, where they caught Royston in one of his now increasingly rare down moments prompted mainly by the resignation of his

18

assistant. Having learned all she could, she'd gone over to Gibbs and Sons, the opposition in Draymarket, albeit just beyond the fringes of where he reigned supreme. The problem was that she was young, energetic and personable and had made lots of contacts, so a raid into his territory was now a distinct possibility, even though he'd long since come to an understanding with John Gibbs, owner of the rival agency. He looked up as the door opened and Heather and Hannah walked into his life.

Royston always arrived early for appointments and it was just as well he did, since the large green painted and peeling double gates to Albany House took a bit of opening before he could drive in and pull up in front of the property. The sunshine had the effect of making the former rectory look even more shabby and run-down. "Who the hell's going to pay £485,000 for this place and then another £100,000 to put it back together again," he muttered prophetically. Peter and Lynn Squire's arrived late and full of apologies and it did not take them long to look around and come to the conclusion that it was not exactly what they had in mind. They both quickly realised that doing up Albany House would be a major project, involving much time and great expense and they certainly did not have the time. Had it been a case of a little cosmetic work, then that would have been different. Anyway, they'd dined out on the idea and impressed their friends, so now it was time to tiptoe quietly away and say nothing more about it.

Chapter 3

It was over breakfast that Saturday morning that Laura and Ben told the kids about going to look around Albany House and they were quite surprised by their reaction. Lottie seemed as if she was about to burst into tears and Luke, who'd glanced across at his sister, just looked down at his cereal and started pushing it around the bowl with his spoon. Laura's heart went out to them.

"Mummy and Daddy only want to go and have a look. It really is very unlikely that we'll be moving."

Their appointment was for 2.30pm and the children, who normally chatted away ten to the dozen in the back of the family's mid-range and now slightly battered and scratched salon car, were subdued and listened in silence to their parents' occasional comments as they drove through narrow country lanes, flush with the vibrant green of early spring.

The way twisted and turned as it led gently upwards towards Little Oreford, which had grown over the centuries on a wooded plateau just a little below the summit of higher ground in the undulating North Devon landscape.

The small and picturesque village was neatly sheltered
from the prevailing westerly winds, which was probably
why it had established itself there in Saxon times. There
was a Norman church and a scattering of houses and
cottages, huddled around a wide green, together with a
long-closed coaching inn, its large and distinctive double
entrance leading through to a spacious inner court now
completely overgrown with weeds.

Commanding the entrance to the village, if approaching
from Hampton Green, was a substantial four-storey
converted mill.

Its wooden water wheel had disappeared long ago from
its position over the stream flowing gently down from
higher ground. Albany House stood at the far end of the
green and was accessed via a drive overshadowed by
three large beech trees, whose swollen buds were
poised to burst forth onto a new green world, but the
nearer they drew to Laura's dream home, the greater
became her doubt.

Even if they could scrape enough cash together to buy
Albany House, it would probably mean they'd be broke
all the time and then the kids' reaction had tugged at her
heart strings.

Royston was already parked outside the front door and they watched him get out, clipboard in hand, as they drew up beside him on a weed covered gravel drive, which had long since given up the will to crunch.

Both children climbed out reluctantly, but then gazed around in growing awe as they took in the wide expanse of front garden with all the room in the world to play. Hanging limply from the branch of one of the beeches was the remains of a swing on a withered rope and the two bounded over to it. Ben saw its dangers in an instant and chased after them, leaving Royston and Laura standing there. "Luke, Lottie, come back! That swing is bound to be dangerous!" The fear in his voice arrested them and they stopped a few yards short of the dangling rope and stood looking up at where it was secured to a bough. "Well, can we have a new one please?" Luke asked, excitedly.

Laura smiled at Royston as, with her small family gathered around him, he produced a key and pushed open the front door.

They all crowded into the spacious entrance hall, where the first thing Laura noticed was the beautifully carved wooden banister feature staircase giving access to a first-floor landing. 'Wouldn't that look simply wonderful all decorated with winter greenery at Christmas,' she thought. Luke was taken by it too, but only as a super slide.

Royston led the way into a Victorian drawing room with a double window, flower tiled fireplace, plaster reliefs around the ceiling rose and a wooden picture rail. Ben quickly spotted the tell tale damp patches climbing up the walls from the double sized skirting boards, the fashion in Victorian times. Their living room furniture would be totally out of character and lost in this much bigger space, but the type that would suit could be picked up for virtually nothing at salerooms these days, he thought.

Laura was already following Royston back into the hall and then into the rear dining room where the afternoon sun was streaming in through a large and dusty south facing window.

Her spirits rose as if in response to the reflected warmth. While both the drawing and dining rooms were considerably bigger than their own, they were not so large as to make a transition to them unthinkable. She wandered over to the window and peered out through the grime and was delighted to see a wide stone-paved terrace running the whole length of the house. It was surrounded by a low wall and there were steps leading down into the garden, which sloped gently away towards a line of beeches some fifty metres beyond. What once had been a lawn was now little more than a field of waist-high grasses dotted with wild flowers, but a few hours with a strimmer would sort that out.

She turned and followed the others, who'd already entered the kitchen and were gazing silently about them. The floor was covered in an expanse of green linoleum, faded and cracked in a number of places, in the middle of which stood a large table covered by sheets of yellowing newspaper. But what really caught everyone's eye was the ancient Aga standing in a cavernous stone edged fireplace. Full of curiosity, Luke and Lottie advanced on it and began opening its various doors and peering into the blackness. On top was a large blackened kettle, an even larger saucepan and a couple of smaller ones, which was odd seeing that no other traces of domesticity had been left by the previous occupant. Royston turned to the second page of his sales brochure, compiled by one of his girls, and searched for details of the Aga, seeing that the family seemed to be paying it particular attention. "It's solid fuel and I guess those utensils have been left because they'd be useless in a modern kitchen." Laura and Ben had heard about Agas and knew vaguely that using one was completely different from modern gas and electric cookers, where heat was available instantly on demand, but had never confronted one before. A door led outside, but Royston suggested they should finish the internal tour and look at the grounds afterwards.

Even mention of 'the grounds' sounded impressive and would have been totally out of context in Cherry Grove, Ben thought, as they all trooped after the agent back into the hall and up the stairs. Just imagine these lovely wooden banisters all woven with ivy and berries at Christmas, Laura thought again, but kept that to herself. There were four good size bedrooms, two front and back on each side of the central stairway. All had dusty oak floors, again with high skirting boards, and each contained a small fireplace flanked by patterned tiles, below which was a small stone hearth, but what really grabbed the family's attention was the oblong bathroom, sandwiched between the two rear bedrooms. It was dominated by a large cast iron bath at the foot of which loomed an enormous hot water tank. "We could actually swim in it," exclaimed Lottie excitedly. At the far end of the bathroom was a substantial porcelain sink and to the left of it, a toilet with an ancient wooden seat, but what roused the children's interest most was the chain dangling from beside the ornate cast iron overhead cistern. They'd seen one before, but only in a picture. "Let's pull it. Can we dad?" Luke asked looking around at Ben and that official looking man. "Of course, you can, but I'm not sure you can reach it," replied Royston. He was beginning to enjoy showing this family around. He knew he liked kids, but didn't have much experience of them. How different this viewing was from the one earlier.

Luke just managed to reach the chain by standing on tiptoes, but Lottie had to be held up once the cistern had refilled.

Royston noted that the water supply was still on and had better be turned off come winter.

Leaving by the front door, they waited for the agent to lock up before leading the way around the right-hand side of the house. They all wandered out and along the sunlit terrace, weeds surrounding all the flagstones. "I don't think we'll look around the garden," said Ben, surveying the waist high grasses. "Why can't we Dad, just for a few minutes?" challenged Luke, edging his way towards the steps. "No, because you can't see what's underfoot. There could be holes in the ground, broken bricks or glass or anything." Luke scowled. "But I really want to, Dad," he said, edging still further towards the step. "I do too," said Lottie, taking a lead from her brother. "No, and that's my last word," said Ben, ending their small moment of defiance.

Royston was beginning to hope that he might have found buyers for Albany House and it would be a relief to take its picture out of his window. Houses that didn't sell and were unlikely to sell in the current market were anathema to him and there were now too many of them on his books, which worried him.

"Well, what do you think of the property?" he asked, after they had all walked slowly back to their respective cars. Laura glanced at Ben and waited for him to say something. "Is anyone else interested in the house?" he asked casually. "Funnily enough I had a viewing this morning. Another couple from the village as it happened," he admitted. "And what was their response?" Ben asked. "Well, I don't think they'll be proceeding. I think they felt it was a little too much to take on." Ben and Laura looked at each other.

They'd both let reality slip for a few happy minutes and Laura had even begun having second thoughts about her objections to renting from the Squire's, but now even that plan had been quashed and there was no way in the world they could afford to buy. "We'll have to go away and think more about it," Ben stalled, but the sound of his voice told Royston he was unlikely to hear anything more from them.

His spirits were deflated as he drove back to the office, despite it being a perfect afternoon. He'd rather hoped he was going to find a buyer for Albany House and that all seemed to have come to nothing but, far worse than that, a Gibbs' agency board had gone up right in the middle of his patch and now there was one, just how long would it be before there were two and then three and four? Equally galling was the fact that while his 'Royston Randall' sale boards were a tasteful green and black, those of Gibbs and Sons were a horrible bright red with black lettering and were definitely more eye-catching then his own.

Chapter 4

Laura and Ben both felt disheartened and were wrestling with their feelings, while their children were literally bouncing up and down with excitement at the thought that they might be moving to Albany House. "Are we really going to be moving there, Mum and Dad?" asked Luke. "Yes, are we?" chimed in Lottie. Laura turned around in her seat. "Look, children, we did say we were just going to look and that was really all, so, bearing in mind the huge amount of work that would have to be done, Dad and I don't really think it's an option, not at the moment anyway." So, did that mean they might one day, Luke pressed? "No, probably not," she said gently, but now Ben came to the rescue. "Look kids, you both need new shoes, so why don't we drive over to The Allway Centre and after doing our shopping we could have a pizza."

They got home around 7pm and once the kids were in bed, Laura and Ben poured themselves a large glass of a good white wine and dipped into a tub of mixed olives, bought as a consolation treat. "Well, I guess that's that then, although it was a nice dream while it lasted," sighed Laura, but Ben was still hanging doggedly on to it, at least for the moment. "If the Squire's aren't going to buy Albany House, then maybe we could rent it from the owner, seeing it's highly unlikely to sell any time soon," he suggested. "I suppose I could pop in to Randall's and ask the question," she agreed.

Royston normally spent Sundays washing and polishing his prized sports car while listening to the radio and then taking it out for a spin, but this morning he couldn't settle to it. The vision of that red and black Gibbs' sign kept dancing around in the back of his mind. He knew Heather and Hannah were both in the office and perfectly capable of handling any business which might come in, but somehow being at home was like fiddling while Rome burned. At last, he could stand it no longer, throwing the soapy sponge into its bucket with a splash and going inside to change into his suit.

His appearance in the office took the girls completely by surprise. "Goodness Boss. Have you forgotten it's Sunday?" asked Hannah, glancing up from her paper scattered desk and being immediately struck by the bleak look on his face. Heather, hearing the conversation, came out from the inner office to see what was going on. She too instantly picked up on Royston's demeanour. "Is everything all right?" she asked.

suddenly seized by the fear that he was about to make them redundant.

"You asked me what's up, so I'm going to show you," he said, turning and heading back towards the door. Both girls, now wondering what on earth was going on, abandoned their desks and followed him out onto the pavement, as he set off purposefully along the street. Heather paused to flip over the 'closed' sign and hurried after Hannah. Two minutes later, Royston stopped at the corner and pointed along the side road. "That's what's up," he said pointing at the Gibbs' sign. Both his assistants gasped as they clocked the garish red and black 'For Sale' board.

"How dare they?" hissed Hannah, feeling anger welling up inside her. "This is war!" declared Heather vehemently. The two had grown to love their kind hearted and considerate Boss as a sort of father figure. After all, he'd taken them both on when he'd only really needed one assistant and that had allowed them to escape city life, but now he was upset and they were not going to stand for that. There was another side to the pair, who had the matching temperaments of she-devils if provoked, and now they were provoked! They turned and marched back to the office with Royston trailing a little behind and feeling gratified they had so quickly sprung to his defence. "We must take the fight to them, Boss, by actively and openly seeking new clients in and around Draymarket," said Heather, when they were all seated, but before he could answer a couple walked in and distracted them.

Both girls had viewings booked for the afternoon, so there wasn't really much point in him hanging around. "Before I go, I want to say how much I appreciate your reaction on seeing that Gibbs' board, so enjoy your day off tomorrow and perhaps after work on Tuesday we might have supper at The Lion and consider seriously what we should do about it." They smiled at him.

"OK by us, Boss," said Hannah, looking across at Heather.

Back at his desk on Tuesday morning, Royston saw Laura Jameson and her children passing by on their way to school, but was more than a little surprised when she entered the office some ten minutes later and requested another viewing! "We can go now if you like," suggested Royston, who'd not really expected to see her in his office again and was beginning to hope there might be a sale in prospect after all.

"No, I'll drive myself, so I'll just pop home and pick up the car and meet you there in half an hour."

Surprisingly, she was the first to arrive, so she got out and opened the gate and was just about to drive in when a movement caught her eye and she glanced across to see an older woman with a dog disappearing from view, over to her left. Half hidden in the hedge she spotted a 'public footpath' sign and was wondering where it might lead when Royston drove up behind her and followed her in. Again, they wandered from room to room with Laura asking a series of more searching questions about whether the fire places were still useable and if mains gas was available, as there was no mention of it in the brochure, and what were the rates likely to be?

When, at last, they'd emerged and Royston had locked the front door, she asked him if it was at all likely that the vendor might agree to rent the house to them for two years, by which time the market might have reached his required sale price. He said he'd certainly pass their request on, but privately he didn't think there was a snowball's chance in hell that Anthony Allen would ever agree.

Laura pulled up just outside the gates after he'd gone, as she'd decided to go for a wander around Little Oreford to get more of a feeling for the place. It was another sunny morning, so she wandered to the middle of the green and stopped and looked all around her. For some curious reason, the rusty sign still hanging limply from iron stanchions over the inn door was the first to arrest her wandering gaze.

Immediately opposite, was a pair of attractive detached thatched cottages, rising up from behind a waist-high stone wall. One was rendered white and the other of exposed stone with a mass of wisteria vines rambling all over it. To her far left, where the lane entered the village, stood the old mill house. whose large imposing outer wall cast a deep shadow over the narrow road, unless the sun was more or less directly overhead. The building's lower floors were hidden behind the wall and a set of six-foot-high wooden gates. It was known to locals as 'The Corner House' because, to its right, was a lane trailing off towards the church, whose telltale spire could be seen rising above a substantial row of trees. There do seem to be a lot of beeches around here, which makes the place seem just a little closed in, but still a delight, she thought, turning around to see the woman she'd spotted by the footpath sign earlier, now walking towards her with a dog on the lead.

"Are you coming to live in Albany House?" she asked. Laura suddenly felt embarrassed, and replied that she'd certainly like to. "I'm Margo and this is Tiff," the older woman said, looking down at her small black poodle. "My brother, Robin, and I live in the white cottage over there and we spotted you and your family looking around the house on Saturday, when we were out walking, and, to tell you the truth, it raised our hopes, because we'd so love to see the dear old place lived in again. Look, have you got time to come in for a coffee, seeing that we might soon be neighbours?" she asked. "I certainly wouldn't raise your hopes on that score, but yes I'd love a coffee," replied Laura.

The beautifully furnished cottage was much larger than it first appeared from the outside and had an extensive back garden with a central lawn that would do justice to any bowling green, surrounded by well stocked herbaceous flower borders.

"This is lovely," said Laura, as she was led out through open French windows and invited to take a seat at the patio table. "Robin, we have a visitor," called Margo and with that, a tall man in baggy green corduroy trousers, an open neck white shirt and battered straw hat appeared from a large pagoda style greenhouse to her left. "I won't shake hands because I've been mixing compost," he said, sitting down opposite her, while Margo went to make the coffee.

The two, now in their early sixties, had, Robin explained, moved to Little Oreford with their parents when they were children. Laura suddenly thought of Luke and Lottie, who might be following in their footsteps a life time later. "Albany House was still the rectory in those days and we soon made friends with the Rev Potter's children, Cynthia and Charlie, who were around our own age," Robin recalled wistfully, his mind flashing back to those always sunny childhood days. "Cynthia was shy and quite introverted, but Charlotte, who Insisted on being called Charlie, was a real tomboy.

We all spent most of our summers roaming around the fields and woods, climbing trees, building dens, fishing and having camp fires. We'd often go off after breakfast with a pack of sandwiches and not get back till teatime and nobody gave it a second thought; not like today when most parents won't let their children out of their sight."

Margo, who'd returned and was serving the coffee, said it was a completely different world now and that parents couldn't be blamed for being protective. Laura couldn't

37

help thinking she was right, but kept her opinion to herself. "So, are we going to have you as neighbours then?" Robin asked. Laura flushed at being suddenly put on the spot again. "We'd love to, but to be honest, we certainly couldn't afford to buy the house and while my husband, Ben, is quite keen to rent it, I'm really in two minds, because while moving here was all my idea, the thought that we'd never be able to make any real improvements, because it wasn't ours, is putting me off," she admitted. "Do you think you might be able to rent it?" Robin asked. "I don't know. It's probably a non-starter, but the estate agent is finding out for us," she said glancing at her watch. "Goodness, is that the time? I really must be going. It's been lovely talking to you and enjoying your wonderful garden." As they reached the front door, Margo said she'd ask Robin to dig out some old photographs of Albany House and the Rev Potter and his family in what were probably the last of its heydays in the 1950's "We're around on Thursday morning if you'd like to come for another coffee and we'll have found the pictures by then." Without thinking, Laura said she'd love to.

Chapter 5

Royston shut up shop promptly at 5.30pm on the following Tuesday and the three of them walked over to The Red Lion, all glancing sideways as they passed the end of the road to see the Gibbs sign still in place and mocking them. "We'll show them," muttered Hannah. "Look what the wind just blew in, Pet," said Geoff, the landlord, who was busy polishing a wine glass when they entered. His wife looked up and broke into a broad smile. "It's The Demons. This isn't Thursday is it, Geoff?" Royston, who was only an occasional visitor, looked puzzled. "We always do the pub quiz on Thursdays, but they don't let us play together anymore," complained Heather. "Too right, we don't. They're practically unbeatable together and it takes all the fun out of it for everyone else," said Geoff. "That's what comes of being sad little book worms and previously working in a library," said Hannah. Royston asked them what they wanted and as it was red wine all round, he bought a bottle and ordered some breads and olives as a starter. He'd made up his mind he was going to treat them to a good dinner.

They settled themselves around a corner table at the back of the bar and the girls waited expectantly for their boss to open the discussion. "This sale board might just be a one-off, because the vendor happened to be friends with someone at Gibbs.

That does happen sometimes," said Royston, explaining that for years there had been an understanding between his firm and Gibbs and Sons that they wouldn't seek instructions in each other's areas. Both agencies had their own pages in the Draymarket Gazette, but while John Gibbs covered the town and looked east, Randall's operated west towards the North Devon coast. "Boss has a point that this probably is a one-off, so why don't we draw up a contingency plan, which we can act on if one board should become two?" suggested Heather.

It amused Royston that they never called him Royston only ever 'Boss.' The plan they devised over dinner was to place a full-page advert in The Gazette, advertising a one per cent commission fee for all Draymarket instructions for a limited period, followed the next week by a flyer inside the paper. They would at the same time look for some temporary premises to rent, which one of them would staff on Fridays, Saturday's and Sunday's.

The following afternoon, Laura was standing with her friend Sarah, waiting for their children to come out of school, when she got an embarrassing surprise. "No school tomorrow. No school tomorrow," Luke and Lottie and their friends, Oliver and Andrew, chanted as the foursome skipped happily towards their mums. She turned to her friend, a puzzled look on her face. "Don't say you've forgotten it's an in-service training day!" Yes, Laura had forgotten and then she remembered her promise to go and have another coffee with that lovely couple in Little Oreford. She was about to ask Sarah if she'd look after Luke and Lottie for a couple of hours, but then stopped herself.

She always seemed to be asking her friend to have her kids, so this time she'd have to sort her mistake out by taking her children with her. As they passed Randall's, Laura decided on impulse to call in and see if there was any news, but there was none. Anthony Allen it seemed, never answered his telephone, so one could only leave a message, and if he didn't like what he heard, then he would simply ignore it, or at least that was Royston's reading of the situation. "I've written setting out your case as positively as I could, but whether he'll trouble to answer is anyone's guess, Mrs Jameson."

On the drive through sunlit lanes up to Little Oreford the following morning, Laura did her level best to contain the children's excitement. "No, we can't go and look around the house again, because we haven't got an appointment, and I'm not saying that we'll be invited into the cottage, so please calm down."

Laura pulled up outside Margo and Robin's cottage and told Luke and Lottie to stay in the car while she went and knocked on the door, but it opened before she got there because Margo had been watching out. "Of course, the children can come in. They can be playmates for Robin and Tiff while we chat," she said, leading them through into the garden.

Fine bone china cups for three with linen napkins in silver rings beside the plates had already been carefully laid out on the patio table, making Laura feel even more embarrassed that she'd come with the kids. "Robin, we have visitors. Where are you?"

Her brother, still in his baggy green corduroy trousers and now not quite so white, open neck shirt, promptly appeared from around the side of the house followed by Tiff, who bounded towards them. "Robin, Tiff, these are Laura's children, Luke and Lottie, and they've been allowed to escape from school because it's an in-service

42

training day." Robin smiled. "Excellent, I was always doing my best to escape from school." He had such a kindly face, they both took to him in an instant. "Tell you what, Robin, why don't you take Luke and Lottie to see what you've been working on for months?" The children were instantly intrigued and looked up at their mum to see if it would be all right. "Go on then and perhaps I can come and see later." But it was to be much sooner than later, because she and Margo had hardly sat down when both offspring came running back across the lawn in high excitement. "Mum, you must come and see; you must!" Laura looked at her hostess, who was smiling. "Come on then. We'll all come and see," laughed Margo. With that, the children were racing back from whence they had come with the two following and chatting. Suddenly turning, her host led the way along a narrow path through the herbaceous border and into a side garden, where the reason for her children's excitement was instantly obvious. There, in front of her, was a complete model village, but not just any model village. It was Little Oreford clearly back in much earlier times and exquisite in every detail. Laura's first impression was that the village, which she'd thought was little more than an overgrown hamlet, looked much bigger from the air and

43

had a wider scattering of houses than could be seen from the green.

""Look, Mum, there's the tree in the front garden of our new house, only the swing's missing," said Luke. "Well, after we've had some refreshments, why don't you two help me make another one?" suggested Robin, standing like a friendly giant over his creation, clearly delighted at the children's response.

Leading the way, he entered a large stone building with a tiled roof, the interior of which was surrounded by work benches strewn with small tools, pots of paint, tubes of glue, small rolls of fine wire, balls of string, half-finished structures, and much else. "Wow," was all Laura could say while the children, now gathered themselves protectively by her side, just looked about them.

"Come on then, let's go and get some drinks," said Margo, breaking the spell, and they all followed her back up the garden to the patio.

"My brother's been researching the history of Little Oreford for some years," said Margo, after Robin and the children had gone back to his workshop. "It was after he'd collected quite a few old photographs that he was suddenly inspired to create a model of the village as it was in the early 1900s," she explained.

They'd been left the cottage when their parents died, but only came together to occupy it some ten years earlier, after their early retirements coincided by design, she explained. Margo said Robin had risen through the ranks of the Civil Service to become a parliamentary private secretary and, being wedded to his occupation, had never found time to be married. She'd had several long term relationships, which in the end had come to nothing, so she'd also concentrated on her career, eventually becoming head of her county library service. The church clock was striking noon before she knew it, and glancing down at her watch, she wondered just where the morning had gone. "Look If you don't have anything on this afternoon, why don't you all stay for a sandwich lunch, because we haven't even looked at those pictures yet?" Laura said she'd hate to impose, but Margo was not taking 'no' for an answer.

After lunch, the children disappeared with Robin back to the workshop where, having finished and put up the tiny swing, they were now helping to make a section of fencing.

Margo went inside and emerged with an old leather-bound picture album, which instantly transported them, time traveller like, back to a long forgotten black, white and sepia world.

There were several dozen pictures of people standing outside houses and of scenes, not immediately identifiable, as well as a few postcards from the 1890's showing the cottages around the green, an open-topped charabanc crowded with people in their Sunday best outside the inn, and a couple of St Michael's Church, but the ones which naturally captivated Laura were those of Albany House. The first was clearly of a garden party, probably again around the turn of the last century, with people seated at a scattering of tables along the terrace and below on a manicured lawn overlooking open country sloping gently away into the distance. "But there are no views from the terrace now, only of woods at the bottom of the garden," said Laura. "That's why there are none in Robin's model, if you go and have another look," replied Margo, now turning over the page to reveal another picture of the terrace, but this time from the early1950's.

"Here's Robin and me with the last rector, Will Potter, his wife, Anne, and their two children, who were our best friends."

Laura was only half listening because there was something disturbingly familiar about Mrs Potter. "Don't you think she looks just like me?", she said. Margo picked up the album and took a closer look. "Wait a moment. I'll get Robin's magnifying glass."

There was, they quickly realised, an almost unnerving resemblance, between Laura and the dark short-haired pixy-like image staring back at them from across the years. "This is really weird, because when I first met you on the green, you looked vaguely familiar and I couldn't think why. So, what an amazing coincidence."

Laura decided not to dwell on the likeness, but then it occurred to her that perhaps something more than a childhood story book picture had drawn her to Albany House. "Are you still in touch with your two childhood friends?" she asked. "No. We all went our separate ways and Robin and I only found out what had happened to the family during our visits home to see our parents. It wasn't a very happy story because Cynthia, the older daughter, never left home and sadly died from cancer in her early forties and apparently the Rev Potter never really got over it. Charlie went off to Bristol University, got pregnant and fell out with her family and no one seems to know what happened to her after that. Her

47

father died in his late eighties, but her mother lived on in the house until she passed away in her mid-nineties, after which the property was inherited by Anthony Allen, a distant relative, who was living overseas and did nothing for some years until his return to the UK last autumn," said Margo.

"No wonder poor old Albany House is in such a sorry state and no one wants to take it on except us and we can't afford it, at least not at the moment that is." Laura said it seemed a shame that their childhood friend should have fallen out with her parents, especially when she was pregnant, and had not gone on to inherit the old rectory. "I think there must have been far more to it than that, but I guess we'll never know now," said Margo, closing the album on her lap and laying it back on the coffee table. "Thank you so much for showing me," said Laura. "But there are two things I must say before we go. The first is that there's really very little chance of us coming to live in Little Oreford at the moment, unless Mr Allen will rent it to us, which doesn't seem likely," she admitted. "And what's the second?" asked Margo. "We've all had such a lovely time with you today that I was wondering if you and Robin would like to come around for tea on Sunday afternoon?"

The children were high as kites on the way home, but Laura was lost in her own world. It really was quite weird how she had been so attracted to Albany House and then to discover that she looked so much like Anne Potter. It was almost as if the woman was somehow drawing her to Little Oreford from beyond the grave. But while that was slightly unsettling, she still had an extremely warm feeling about the house and somehow knew that Anne Potter's influence, if indeed such a thing could be possible, was of a benign nature. But then there had also been that odd incident the morning she'd gone to The Allway Centre to buy the fish for their dinner party.

Happening to glance sideways along the aisle, she'd spotted another young woman, who also looked remarkably like her. For a moment their eyes had met and Laura instinctively turned away in embarrassment, but when she looked back, the other woman had gone.

Chapter 6

It was around 4pm on the day after Laura and the children had been up to Little Oreford, that a woman, probably in her late 30's, entered Randall's looking for somewhere to rent.

Miss Alicia Wiltshire had recently joined the teaching staff at the village primary school and was staying with friends in Draymarket, while she found somewhere to live. There was an air of quiet sophistication about Miss Wiltshire. She was slim, of slightly above average height, with shoulder length blonde hair and fine features, who didn't look to Royston to be the sort who could handle a class of thirty or so, boisterous eight-year-olds.

"It would be ideal if I could find somewhere hereabouts and not have to drive to school every day," she explained. "I know it's probably a long shot, but I thought it was worth enquiring just in case." Royston said he'd nothing at the moment, but would keep her contact details on file and certainly let her know if something did turn up. His eyes followed her appreciatively as she left and then he turned back to his laptop to make a fresh entry.

As it was quiz night at The Lion, Hannah and Heather had got into the habit of going straight there from work and having a bite to eat while they waited. "Tell you what," said Hannah, after they'd ordered and were sitting down with a couple of glasses of house white, "I think Boss fancied Miss Alicia Wiltshire. Did you notice the way he looked after her as she left?" Heather hadn't noticed, but agreed their boss had been a little more attentive than was usual. Just why Royston was single had often puzzled the two ever since they'd come to work for him.

They both agreed he probably wasn't gay, but more likely to be painfully shy, as far as women were concerned. He had his business, his beloved vintage sports car and his secretarial role with its regional owners' club to keep him occupied. So perhaps he was biding his time and just waiting for Miss Right to come along. "Well, if you are right, Han, and he is interested in Miss Wiltshire, then what could we do to further this relationship?" They could start right away by finding out a little more about her from the three or four parents, who were normally at the quiz, Heather suggested.

As it turned out, Royston had spent that evening attending a meeting of the owners' club in Tiverton and it

51

was dark on the final leg of his drive home to his bungalow, just outside Yardley Upton. But his good mood evaporated the closer he got to home, because there was still no special person with whom to share his life. Everyone in his small circle was with someone, but he had no one and, while normally he could brush these occasional feelings of loneliness aside, there were times like this when a sadness stole over him and he knew, from past experience, that it would be some time before it melted away. Just a small thing, like standing next to a couple unloading their trolley at a supermarket till, would recall his loneliness into sharp focus from its blurred presence at the back of his mind.

 "Get a grip," he muttered, suddenly depressing the accelerator, and feeling the power surge, and in that split second a small deer appeared in the glare of his headlights. Braking violently as the sports car hit an extended patch of mud outside a farm gate, he lost control.

Slewing half sideways across the road, the car smashed through a hedge and piled its front end into an ivy covered and half-rotten tree and everything went black. Slowly, he began regaining consciousness, becoming aware first that his body was somehow contorted in a confined space and that he couldn't see anything and then, in a flash, he knew where he was and what had happened. 'If the car catches fire you'll be burned alive in seconds.' The terrifying thought sent him into a panic and he began struggling, but it was useless. Then he realised that while he couldn't move his body, his left arm seemed to be free. It also occurred to him that he wasn't in any pain, so maybe he was OK. 'Think, Royston, think.' It was as if his late father was speaking to him from across the years. It was a phrase he'd often used when chiding his son about something stupid he'd done without really thinking. Then he realised his mobile phone might still be in the glove compartment, where he always deposited it. Stretching tentatively forward to where he thought the compartment should be, his hand came up against some hard surface. "This is bloody useless," he muttered in the darkness and in that moment a full moon, suddenly emerging from a chink in the clouds, filtered light down through the branches and he was instantly aware of his position.

The whole front of the car had been smashed in, leaving him squashed in his seat, while the vehicle was hemmed in on both sides by the thick hawthorn he'd crashed through. Then all was darkness again. If the back of the car was still sticking out into the road, then the next person coming along was going to spot him, he reasoned. But what if it wasn't?

He could be there all night, or even longer, much longer! The thought was horrifying and again he felt a rising fear beginning to sweep away the sober reasoning that had been his previous, and now short-lived, state of mind. "Hell, how much have I had to drink, because I'm bound to be breathalysed when the emergency services turn up?" he asked himself. The random thought again fuelled his panic as he began thinking of the consequences of losing his licence. Then he heard a car approaching and prayed its driver would spot him and, thank God, the vehicle appeared to be slowing down. Becoming acutely aware of a bright light coming from behind him, he heard a door open and footsteps approaching.

"Is anyone there?" It was a woman's voice. "Yes, I'm here and trapped in my car," he shouted. "Are you OK?" she asked, "Yes, I think so, but I just can't move."

She sounded young and she told him told not to worry because she was going to call for help. Her headlights shining through the hedge at an angle and restricted by all the greenery, cast a dull light into the car and Royston saw instantly that chunks of his windscreen were still hanging around the edges, like minute pieces of crazy paving. The dashboard appeared to have caved in and was preventing him from moving. "I've called the emergency services and they'll be here shortly. Are you sure you are OK?" He liked the sound of her voice. "Yes, but I'm trapped by the dashboard. It's pinning me back in my seat." There was a pause.

 "I can't get any closer because the hedge is really thick on both sides of your car, but don't worry, I'll stay here till help comes." Royston said he was sorry for all the trouble he was causing her. "Please don't worry about that," she said.

There was another longer pause as they both wondered how to continue the conversation. "I guess I'm certainly messing up your evening," said Royston. "Seems to me that you're the one whose evening's been messed up!" she replied. "You're right about that," Royston shouted back, thinking it had been a bit unkind of her to state the obvious.

Her mobile phone started ringing, its chirpy tune, rudely filling the silence between them. She answered it and as she did so, Royston became aware of the comforting sound of a rapidly approaching siren. It only seemed like

55

a couple of minutes since they'd been called, so perhaps, he'd blacked out again. "Thank God for that," he said, vocalising a huge sense of relief. Then he heard a second siren and wondered whether that might be an ambulance, or the police. The crash site was quickly bathed in light and he heard someone forcing a passage between the side of the car and the hedge. Within seconds, another officer, flashlight in hand, had found an alternative way into the woodland and was standing in front of the car and peering in at him through the shattered windscreen.

"Don't worry we'll have you out of there soon enough," he replied, after Royston had confirmed he was all right. But then, sweeping his beam around the scene, the fireman quickly spotted that a half-rotten tree trunk was now tilting ominously forward over the car.

What had simply seemed like a case of releasing Royston and towing his vehicle slowly backwards out of the hedge, was now far more complicated. Had they attempted any manoeuvre, it seemed highly likely the tree would come crashing down onto the vehicle.

The concerned, but calm face of a paramedic appeared in the jagged space where the windscreen had been and, again Royston confirmed he was OK as far as he could tell.

It started raining and he could vaguely see the moisture in the glare of the lights flooding the scene. It took over an hour for his rescuers to secure the tree, cut him free and tow out the smashed- up car, by which time he was feeling cold, extremely tired, weak and desperate to relieve himself, which he promptly did by staggering off into the shadows. Just how he'd managed to hold on without wetting himself he'd never know, but it had certainly concentrated his mind. Royston was gently escorted to a waiting ambulance and helped up into it, at which point a police officer appeared and asked him to blow into a breathalyser tube. A few anxious moments later, he'd tested negative and the ambulance drove off, but Royston quickly realised that, apart from a small cut on his head and some quite nasty bruising to both legs, he was actually in one piece.

The hospital Accident and Emergency Department was experiencing yet another busy night, so borrowing a mobile phone, he called a taxi, which took an age to come, and eventually reached home around 3.30am. His house key was on the same ring as his car keys and what had become of them, he had no idea, but he had a spare concealed for emergencies and let himself in and crashed out on his bed.

The constant ringing of his house phone woke him to a sunlit room and he rolled over and fumbled for the receiver, realising as he did that he was still fully dressed and that the sleeve of his jacket was crumpled and covered in dirt. Where that had come from, he had no idea and then he remembered the accident. "Is that you, Boss?" It was Hannah and she sounded concerned. "It's way past 10am and we were getting worried about you, seeing you had a viewing at 9.30am, but don't worry, Heather's covered it," she told him. "Sorry, Han. I had a late one and I've overslept, which is most unlike me." He purposely avoided mentioning the accident, because he knew that would have resulted in a whole barrage of concerned questions and he didn't have the energy to get involved in all of that. "I'm really glad you called, because, goodness knows, what time I'd have woken up, but look I'm still not feeling too brilliant, so I'll see you this afternoon." He ran a bath, took a long and contemplative soak, cursing himself for having taken his sports car and not his office motor and vowing to forget all about finding a woman.

A watery sun was shining as he drove slowly down the lane towards the scene of the accident and quickly spotted the large gap in the hedge, where his beloved sports car had been. Beyond was a layby and a farm gate. He pulled into it, stopped, and got slowly out, as if he was somehow reluctant to face the reality of what had happened.

The water filled ruts at the field entrance explained it all and he wondered vaguely if the farmer might be liable for not cleaning the mud from his tractor wheels off the road, but dismissed the idea. Let's face it; he'd been going too fast.

Walking slowly back, he peered guiltily through the gap he'd made in the hedge, but didn't venture any further until he'd returned to the car, opened the boot and donned the green wellies that always lived there.

The first piece of debris he spotted on entering the crash site was his registration plate, which the vehicle recovery people had obviously missed in the darkness. He picked it up, turned it face up and looked at it. "You bloody fool," he muttered bitterly as, seeing no other obvious remains, he turned and walked back to the car. Reaching into his dark blue jacket pocket, it was definitely a sombre suit day, he retrieved the scrap of paper, he'd placed there, containing the telephone number of the community officer, who'd breathalysed him. Then, pulling out his reserve pay-as-you-go mobile, he called what turned out to be the regional control room. After some explanations and several conversations, he eventually obtained the telephone number of the breakdown and recovery firm that had collected his car, because it was obstructing the highway, and said he would be with them shortly. Their yard was tucked away on a small industrial estate close to Draymarket, and also the base for an adjoining car body shop, a tyre centre and several small engineering and other workshops.

The general view of those in the body shop and the recovery people, who'd already made a cursory inspection, but had failed to find his mobile, was that, as the vehicle was over ten years old and its bonnet had caved in, his insurers would write it off. However, they thought it could probably be repaired. Royston mulled over his options as he paid the recovery bill and then decided to have his sporty run around repaired. It'll be costly, but it'll be my punishment,' he rationalised.

It was around 3pm when he finally pushed open their office door and as Hannah looked expectantly up from her desk, he realised he didn't feel at all well and should really have given himself a couple more days off. "Boss, whatever's happened to you?" Her voice was full of concern as she spotted the plaster on his left temple and saw how tired and drawn he looked. He made for his desk, sat down heavily in his padded swivel chair and told her all that had happened. "You're probably suffering from delayed shock, so you must go straight back home and rest and leave everything to Heather and I for a couple of days." Royston needed no further bidding. He drove slowly home and went straight to bed and dozed fitfully for some hours. He was now running a temperature and had a vague feeling of soreness in his throat. It was probably a delayed reaction to becoming thoroughly chilled during the rescue operation and again he cursed himself for being so bloody reckless as to lose control of his car. Then he was thinking about the rescue and it occurred to him that he really needed to thank the woman, who'd spotted the car sticking out of the hedge and had raised the alarm. Suddenly motivated by a sense of purpose, he got slowly out of bed, put on his dressing gown and slippers, and padded into his study, but he quickly discovered he wasn't going to obtain the name of his mystery saviour from the police or the emergency services due to data protection. He'd clearly have to find some other way of contacting her, or alternatively forgetting all about it, because, after all, she'd only dialled 999 from her mobile as anyone else would have done.

Ben Jameson wasn't pleased at the prospect of playing host to the elderly couple from Little Oreford on his precious Sunday afternoon, but sensed that Laura, and particularly the kids, would be really disappointed if he objected, so he kept his feelings to himself. He'd been doing a lot of that lately as pressures on his working life at the hospital seemed to go on increasing with every week which flew by in a haze of bed and staff shortages and a myriad of other issues. To add to that, it now looked very much as if they were going to be sued over a bungled surgical procedure, which they might have to settle out of court at heaven knows what cost. The trouble was that Ben now felt trapped because the chances of him finding another job outside the hospital with equal pay, were pretty slim. He could always go to their GP and get signed off for a couple of weeks on the grounds of stress, but that would only be leaving his already hard-pressed colleagues to cope and the amount of work which would have accrued in his absence would be horrendous. They were getting by on his salary, but only just and the pot was invariably empty by the time his next monthly salary was paid in.

They'd always agreed that Laura should give up her bank cashier's job once the children came along, but now, he was seriously wondering if he should suggest that she might look for a part-time job to help make ends meet.

But Margo and Robin's Sunday afternoon visit turned out to be a most pleasurable diversion and he actually stopped thinking about the hospital for a change. They came armed with books for the children and a pot of homemade raspberry jam for Laura and he saw instantly how the couple had already bonded with his family. Luke couldn't wait to take Robin up to his bedroom to show him the model village he'd already started making out of Lego bricks and Lottie was delighted with her story book. They had only come for tea, but stayed for early supper and for a drink after the children had eventually been persuaded to go to bed.

"We both always wanted children, but somehow it never happened for either of us did it, Robin?" said Margo after a third glass of wine. "No, I guess it wasn't to be life's path for us, Margs," Robin agreed. "Well, it seems to me you've got a couple of surrogate ones now," replied Ben looking across at Laura. "Our two have no hands-on grandparents because my parents sadly died when I was young and Ben's are half a world away in Sydney."

It was some weeks later that Margo happened to glance out of her bedroom window to see two cars, followed by a white van, stop at the entrance to Albany House and then disappear down the drive.

Robin was out, so hurrying downstairs and calling Tiff, she quickly put on her boots, grabbed her jacket and his lead, crossed the green and headed for the footpath beside the house. The cars had pulled up outside the now open front door and the van had stopped just inside the gate, she noticed as she lingered for a few seconds before continuing her walk. The path curved left and through a small cops of ash trees, which had grown up at the back of the property, but there were a couple of places where a walker could glimpse a view of the house. Margo stopped, put Tiff on the lead, fished in her pocket for the small pair of bird watching binoculars, which lived there, and pressed forward to get the best possible view. She was instantly rewarded by the sight of a man and a smartly dressed woman standing on the terrace with what looked like a clipboard in her hand. "I don't like the look of this, Tiff." Margo had become very territorial over Albany House, for which she and Robin had so many happy childhood memories, and was where their young friends should be living. From there, the footpath roughly followed around the boundary of the village to emerge in the churchyard and was crossed by another path leading gently down through the fields to Yardley Upton. She decided to complete the circuit and by the time she was walking back across the green towards Albany House, the cars and the van had disappeared, but there, right beside the gate, was a large red and black Gibbs and Sons 'For Sale' board. Margo's instant reaction was to march over and tear it down, but then she thought better of it. "Robin can do it tonight when it's dark," she muttered turning on her heels and hurrying back to the cottage and getting straight on the phone to Laura.

"I wonder if our estate agent knows about this, Margo, and why he didn't put his board up outside the house. I'll leave for school ten minutes early and pop in to Randall's," she said.

Royston, Hannah and Heather were all in the office and looked up as she came through the door. No, they didn't know about the Gibbs' board and had been specifically instructed by the vendor not to put up their own. Royston said he would again call Anthony Allen on her behalf and try to find out if he would let the property. She thanked him, but it was as if she'd tossed a grenade into their office as she closed the door behind her.

"The bastard," muttered Heather. "Don't you mean the bastards, not forgetting Gibbs and Sons?" responded Hannah, "This is war, Boss!" Royston said they should all calm down and take a step back because, as a friend had once advised him, it was best not to get mad, but to get even.

After supper that evening, Margo and Robin recharged their glasses with their favourite French white and wandered out onto the patio to sit and watch the sun go down. "You don't really want me to go out and vandalise that wretched sign, do you Margs?" he asked. She sat silently for a few moments. "No, because I've had a much better idea and to tell you the truth, I've been turning it over in my mind for a while now." A blackbird's familiar evening call from her nest in the boundary hedge, suddenly filled the silence. "You know it would be lovely if the Jameson's were able to move in to Albany House, so why don't we buy it and rent it to them?

We've got all that money just sitting there in the bank, which we never touch because our pensions more than suffice, so what better use could we find for some of our capital?" He gave her a questioning look. "Goodness, I only asked if you wanted me to take that ugly sign down," he countered. "Yes, Brother, but this would be the legal way of doing it and it would be a far better way of investing some of our cash rather than just having it sitting there." Robin slowly toyed with his glass as he mulled the suggestion over in his mind. "I guess my model village has sort of run its course, so doing up Albany House would be a real life-sized project and I bet Laura and Ben and the children would lend a hand." They leaned forward and chinked glasses.

"To Albany House then," they said as one.

Royston, having had the evening to ponder on his earlier heat of the moment vow not to get angry, but to get even, was now having some second thoughts which he voiced to the girls after the coffee had been made and they were all settling in the following morning.

""I've been thinking that perhaps our best course of action would be for me to drive over to Draymarket and ask John Gibbs what's going on and to see if this matter could be settled amicably because, after all, we might be taking a hammer out to crack a nut," he counselled. "No, Boss, because, with the greatest respect, that's not the answer. Han and I talked of practically nothing else last night and we came to the conclusion that we, I mean you," she corrected herself, "need to expand."

"Let's face it, we've not been that busy of late and there's hundreds of houses in and around Draymarket just waiting for us and on top of that, there's a whole new estate being built, or so it says in the Gazette. They've broken your understanding, so now you've got the perfect excuse to expand into Draymarket without feeling guilty about it." Hannah agreed. "If you go over and see John Gibbs and he agrees to honour your understanding, then you might have spared using a hammer to crack a nut, but you'll have shot yourself in the foot instead!" she said. Royston thought about all this for a few moments and was forced to agree they were right. "Yes," said the two, each punching a fist in the air. Shortly afterwards an older couple came into the office and Royston beckoned them to take a seat and enquired how he might be of service. "We'd like to buy Albany House in Little Oreford," said Margo, glancing across at Robin. "We're cash buyers, so we'd like this all to go through as soon as possible, but there's one stipulation

68

in that this transaction must be completed in the strictest confidence with no one, other than yourselves, the vendor and our respective solicitors having any knowledge of it." She hesitated for a moment. "Also, we'd like you to leave your 'For Sale' details in the window for the time being if that wouldn't be a problem and seeing that you now have a sale, would you very kindly call Gibbs and Sons and ask them to leave theirs up as well, if they wouldn't mind?" Royston said he'd never had a request like that before, but it would be OK, while at the same time wondering how Laura Jameson and her husband would take the news when they eventually found out.

The following weeks were extremely busy ones for the Randall's team, who further buoyed up by the totally unexpected sale of Albany House, went all out to put their prepared contingency plan into operation. They placed a series of ads in the Draymarket Gazette announcing their arrival in the town and offering a commission of just one per cent for the first six months of trading and were lucky to find a recently vacated shop in the High Street, which they were able to rent for that period with an option to extend.

It was while Royston was spending the weekend freshening up the new premises with a lick of paint that there was a 'tap' on the glass entrance door and he opened it to admit a smartly dressed man, whom he judged to be in his early forties. "Apologies for troubling you, but I was wondering if you might need the services of a freelance and completely independent mortgage advisor. I'm Sam Mills. I'm new to the area and don't have any ties with any other local agency at the moment." Royston waved him to a seat. "You might well have come at an opportune moment, so perhaps we should adjourn over the road to The Carpenter's Arms, seeing it's almost lunchtime."

True to his profession, Sam was well spoken, with an easy manner and had moved to the area because his wife, a GP, had taken up a partnership with the local practice. It turned out he was also into sports cars, so they immediately got on and spent the lunch hour discussing both cars and the property market.

By the time they shook hands and went their separate ways, it had been agreed that Sam would use the small upstairs office as his base, free of charge, in return for paying Randall's a commission on every new mortgage client they were able to introduce. Better still and by a complete coincidence, he had a personal connection with the national developer poised to begin building the new estate of three hundred homes just outside town and could probably swing it so that Randall's were appointed sole agents.

It had been Royston's original plan to man their new Draymarket office on Friday's, Saturday's and Sunday's, but now he'd decided that one or other of them would be there every day. All was up and running within a fortnight and, true to his word, Sam, who was now ensconced upstairs, introduced Royston to the developer's sales and marketing director, over lunch at The Carpenters. He just happened to be his brother-in-law, and agreed to appoint the firm as sole agents. Royston broke the good news to Hannah and Heather when he returned to the Hampton Green Office later that afternoon. "He told me he had a personal 'in,' but that was the last thing I expected, and what's more, they're happy for us to start selling the two, three, and four bedroom homes off-plan at our new office from next week."

Chapter 7

As May melted into June, work at the hospital didn't get any easier for Ben, but he kept putting off suggesting to Laura that she might start looking around for a part-time job to ease their financial pressures and then it was too late because of the coming school summer holidays.

They had already decided they'd not go away this year, unless it was for a week's camping or to visit a couple of married friends from university days, who now lived with their young son in Weymouth.

They'd just been invited up to Margo and Robin's for the following Saturday afternoon and they were all looking forward to that because they'd not seen the kids' 'adoptive' uncle and aunt for a while, for one reason or another.

The run of long sunny days seemed to be over and a fine drizzle was falling when they pulled up outside Margo and Robin's. Taking off their damp coats and shoes, they made their way into the couple's now familiar lounge, where the kids immediately spotted a large fruit cake making the centrepiece of an afternoon tea spread. There was also a plate piled high with Margo's home-made scones and bowls of strawberry

72

jam and cream. "Honestly Margo, you needn't have gone to so much trouble," Laura reproached gently. "You can't have afternoon tea without cake and scones with jam and cream, can you, children?" said Robin giving Luke and Lottie a wink. "Now there was a special reason for inviting you around this afternoon," said Margo when they'd all finished.

She was looking across at Robin, who was leaning over and retrieving a bulky envelope concealed on a shelf below the table. Laura and Ben exchanged glances, wondering what was going on. "Well, children, shall we ask mum and dad to open it?" he said, handing it over to Laura, who was nearest him.

Taking the envelope in her hands, she looked questioningly at Ben. "Go on, Mum, you open it," said Luke. "Yes, do, Mum," repeated Lottie excitedly. Laura tore open the envelope and slowly took out a set of keys. She looked down at them in complete puzzlement for a few moments and then, in a flash their significance hit her. "Oh my God! They can't possibly be what I think they are, can they?" she said, looking across at Margo and Robin. It was if Ben was watching the whole scene unfolding in slow motion, such was his surprise. "Yes," said Margo. "We've bought Albany House and it would give us the greatest pleasure if the Jameson family would agree to become our tenants." She paused. "Do you think a peppercorn rent of say £100 a month would suffice if Laura and Ben would help us do it up?" she said, looking across at Robin. "Sounds like a good plan to me, but what do you think, Laura and Ben?" Laura just sat looking down at the keys on her lap, in stunned surprise. It was her dream and now it was to come true. "Oh Margo and Robin, what can we possibly say?" she said, turning the heavy set of keys over in her hand and feeling tears welling up in her eyes. "Just say yes," laughed Robin. "Go on, Mum, yes, yes, yes," chorused the kids, now bouncing up and down in their seats. "Honestly, Robin and Margo, I can hardly find the words to tell you just how grateful we all are, because doing up the dear old house will be an amazing project for all of us," she said. "But we'd simply hate to think you had financially burdened yourself for our sakes," she added, suddenly feeling a twinge of guilt. "I think Robin can put your minds at rest with regard to the financial implications," assured Margo.

"It's really quite straightforward," he explained. "When mother died and Margo and I inherited the cottage, we both sold the London homes we'd bought in the late

1960's. Mine, a sizeable Edwardian mews house in central London, went for £4.9 million and Margo's cottage, near the Thames in Richmond, fetched £3.4 million. So all of a sudden, we had over £8 million sitting in the bank and then wisely invested with the assistance of a broker friend of mine from my Cambridge days. So, we've bought Albany House to soak up some of the accrued income and, funnily enough, it's going to be tax advantageous for us anyway," he reassured them. "We both have good pensions and no children or grandchildren of our own, so the money has just been sitting in the background gathering more interest than we'd ever want to spend," he explained. "The thing is," said Margo, "your coming into our lives, right out of the blue, has been a little ray of sunshine, so buying Albany House, which you all so clearly wanted, but would struggle to afford, seemed like the perfect way of saying thank you."

Looking down at the keys, Laura again felt the tears welling up in her eyes. "Oh! Margo and Robin, what can we possibly say other than we are all completely overwhelmed by your generosity.

But it has been a two-way street because we've all loved coming up to Little Oreford and being part of your lives too," she said, giving Margo a spontaneous hug. Ben and Robin got to their feet and shook hands. "I guess that's settled then," said Robin, disappearing into the kitchen and returning with a celebration bottle of Champagne, with orange juice for the children. "To Albany House," he said raising his glass. Everyone chinked glasses. "Yes, to Albany House!" they all cheered.

In that moment, a feeling of huge relief swept over Ben with the realisation that the couple's generosity would give him an opportunity of escaping from the hospital, if indeed, they were being asked to pay such a low rent. Later, while Margo and Laura cleared away the tea, Robin wandered into the lounge with the kids and switched on the TV for the six o'clock news. In an instant, the large screen was filled with a dramatic view of flames and swirling smoke, while the commentary was telling of the latest large-scale bush fires blazing out of control and threatening whole communities in the Australian outback. Then, by sharp contrast, the scene switched to the Arctic and to a huge chunk of frozen white glacier crashing into an ice blue sea. "Is that global warming like we've been told about at school, Uncle Robin?" asked Luke. The two stark scenes, shown on a screen almost twice as big as their one at home, had unsettled him. "Sadly, you are right, but people around the world are now waking up to the dangers of climate change and beginning to do something about it, so everything should be all right in the end," he replied reassuringly.

Luke thought about this for a moment. "I think I'd like to be a scientist and study climate change when I grow up," he declared. Robin said that would be a splendid thing to do, never dreaming the profound effect his throw away comment would have one day. He put on an adventure film for them and he and Margo and Laura and Ben retired to his study to start planning the restoration of Albany House. Shortly into their conversation, Laura said the only thing that was puzzling her was why the 'For Sale' sign was still up in the estate agent's window, even though the house had been sold. "That's because we wanted this to be a surprise, so knowing just how often you've been looking in Randall's window, we realised you'd be straight into the office and asking questions if a 'sold' sign suddenly appeared," explained Margo. "While we're talking about property, what I can't understand is why the inn is closed and looks as if it's been let go," said Ben, suddenly going off on a tangent. "That's easily explained," replied Robin. "It belongs to a family who live miles away and only come a couple of times a year, which is such a shame. Come to think of it, why don't we buy it and reopen it, Margs?" he suggested. "Well, if you do, I'll happily give up the Health Service and come and run it for you," volunteered, Ben. "Don't encourage him," laughed Margo. "Just because we've bought Albany House, he's getting ideas," she scolded.

Laura and Ben spoke little on their way home, because Luke and Lottie would hear every word and become even more excited than they already were.

So they didn't begin discussing their never to be forgotten day until the kids were both asleep in bed, which didn't take long. "This definitely calls for a celebration," said Ben, emerging from their kitchen linked integral garage with the bottle of Champagne they'd been given at Christmas, and joining her on the sagging sofa. After three glasses, Laura was feeling pretty light-headed. "There's also another way we could celebrate darling," she said, laying her head on his shoulder and gently stroking him with her free hand. Later, as they lay in bed and the euphoria of the bubbles had floated away, another thought crept into her mind. "I didn't realise you were so unhappy at work that you'd jump at the chance of giving up your career to go and manage a pub," she ventured. "I was just carried away by the excitement of it all, like we all were, but seeing you've raised it, work has been getting to me lately because of all the pressure," he confessed. "Then why didn't you tell me?" There was a little hurt in her voice. "I intended to a couple of times, but somehow I never got around to it," he admitted. "I wish you could do something else that would be less stressful," she agreed. Ben decided this was the moment to share all that had been on his mind for some weeks. "To tell you the truth, I have been feeling pretty stressed out at work for quite a while now and the problem is, I can't see any end to it," he admitted. "Oh Ben, I do wish you'd shared all this with me before now. I knew something was up, but somehow, and for some stupid reason, I didn't want to put you on the spot. Now it's clear that you're going to have to find something less stressful to do and I'm going to have to go out and get a job!"

He began shaking his head because, while he'd been wondering whether she should do just that, now he was being put on the spot, he was having second thoughts. "Look, we should be able to rent this place out for double the cost of the mortgage, which means I might be able to negotiate cutting my working week down to three and a half days, because our governing trust is still on an economy drive and I don't really think they'd want to let me go." Laura said that was all very well, but knowing him, he'd still try and squash five days' work into three and a half and put himself under even more pressure. "There's absolutely no reason now why, with all the money we'll be saving, you couldn't find something far less stressful to do, while I get a part-time job," she said, suddenly feeling strangely empowered and liberated at the prospect.

Chapter 8

It was also proving to be a momentous day for Royston Randall, who'd been called by his now business rival, John Gibbs, the previous afternoon and invited to pop into his office on the Saturday morning for a chat.

"Well, I guess this is showdown time," Royston said to Hannah and Heather when he'd put the phone down. "But he's the one who reneged on your understanding by starting to operate on our patch and there's nothing he can do about it anyway," declared Heather. "I think I'll reserve judgement until I've heard what John has to say," retorted Royston, who was becoming just a little irritated by the girls' continuing belligerent attitude towards their rival and at the subtle way they'd started bossing him about.

But Royston was an easy going man, who always tried to see the other's point of view, and in that he perceived there was nothing in their behaviour other than a fierce loyalty to him.

John Gibbs had been watching out as Royston approached Gibbs & Son's large double fronted widows, crammed full of homes for sale, and came forward and opened the door.

"Come in, come in, dear boy."

John, who was now in his late 60's, and annoyingly, had a full head of grey hair, while Royston's was receding at the temple, was fond of using that expression if he felt he knew somebody reasonably well. He'd actually known Royston for many years and had established a far closer relationship with his father when he was the proprietor of Randall's estate agency.

But there had been a falling out some time before Royston had stepped into his father's shoes and that was why the two had contrived to steer clear of one another and how it was, that their territorial understanding had come about. Royston was surprised by John's friendly welcome and accepted the offer of a coffee as he was led into an inner office and waved into a comfortable leather chair. They engaged in easy small talk about the town and the state of the market until the coffee had arrived, but once the door had closed behind them John Gibbs wasted little time in coming to the point. "I know your father and I didn't exactly see eye to eye in later years and it soon became clear to me that you felt that quite keenly," he admitted.

"Seeing that your row was probably a contributory factor in his heart attack, then I think you could be right about that," Royston replied, in a tone that was factual rather than confrontational. "Come now, that's a bit unkind after all these years."

Royston immediately regretted it and apologised.

"Apology sincerely accepted," replied John, leaning across the coffee table that separated them and offering the hand of friendship, which Royston accepted.

"So, why have I asked to see you, I expect you are wondering?" Royston said he assumed it was because he'd opened an office down the street. "Well, dear boy, that's right because the truth is, the time has come when I'd rather be out playing golf than sitting in this office. Your opening of a branch in 'my' High Street has forced me to face up to that fact.

Had I been even ten years younger, I'd have willingly taken you on, but the wind has rather gone out of my sails of late and I think it's time to bow out gracefully."

Royston felt a surge of excited anticipation as he asked his rival what, exactly, he was proposing? "I think there are two options, firstly that you buy me out, or secondly that we merge our agencies under the joint name of Randall & Gibbs and I take a back seat."

Royston thanked John, saying he'd given him a lot to think about and that he'd get back to him in a few days, but was pleased they'd now cleared the air and could move forward on the basis of a mutual business friendship. To say he was excited at the prospect of what might lay ahead would be an understatement.

Chapter 9

Laura and Ben spoke little in front of the children about the new life they were beginning to plan. Around noon on the Monday, Laura phoned Margo to invite her and Robin to join them at The Lion for a small thank you celebration supper the following evening. She'd thought about dining at home, but dismissed the idea because, if they'd done so, the kids would definitely not want to go to bed.

Robin had risen early that morning, as was the habit of a lifetime, drew back the curtains and looked out onto the village green and across at the centuries old, former inn, which he now viewed in a new light. In that moment, he was imagining two heavy dray horses drawing up in front, their wagon laden with barrels, and Ben Jameson, the landlord, coming out to meet them.

He went quietly downstairs in his dressing gown, so as not to disturb Margo, who would still be sleeping peacefully. Making his first cuppa of the day, he slipped on his clogs, carried his brew out into the garden, now sodden after a night's gentle rain, and made his way over to his beloved Victorian model village.

Standing there and gazing down at it, he faced up to the fact that this project was completed and that, besides doing up Albany House, making the owners of the former Oreford Inn an offer they couldn't refuse and reopening it, would indeed be an exciting new venture. Then, as if by natural progression, his thoughts moved on to the former mill and substantial house at the end of the green. It was surrounded by a high wall with stout double gates, which were never open, and again owned by absentees, who never went near the place. 'What a waste and why, once they'd reopened the Oreford Inn, should they not also acquire the old mill house and bring it back to life?' he asked himself.

It turned out to be a quiet night at The Lion, which was ideal for Robin and Margo. They were not fans of noisy environments, although he might have to change his view if his plans for reopening the former village inn were ever to become a reality, he told himself.

Laura and Ben arrived shortly afterwards, having walked the children around to Sarah's house for a sleepover, even though it was school the next morning. They ordered drinks and food and then wasted no time in getting down to the initial planning for all the improvements to Albany House. It was agreed the family

86

would move in as soon as the rewiring and installation of the new oil fired central heating system had been completed. But Margo then insisted that she and Robin would employ professional painters and decorators, rather than accepting the couple's offer to do most of the work themselves.

Royston spent most of Tuesday on some initial preparations for his forthcoming merger. By late afternoon, he'd formulated a plan and had concluded a lengthy conversation with his solicitor, who would have to work with the Gibbs' lawyer to draw up a joint agreement acceptable to both parties.

He waited until it was almost going home time before calling John and saying he would be agreeable to a merger, possibly followed later by a buyout, provided the details could be worked out to their mutual satisfaction, and suggesting they should meet up for dinner to talk things over.

That Tuesday was also a memorable one for Laura, who popped into Randall's to see if they could recommend a reliable electrician and heating engineer. She was greeted by Hannah, who assured her that would certainly not be a problem as they also looked after rented properties and had a list of handy people. Laura also broke the news, that she and her husband were going to rent Albany House from their friends, Margo and Robin Lloyd, and would be needing to find a tenant for their home in Cherry Grove. "Then again, you've certainly come to the right place because, only the other day, we had a woman in looking for accommodation in the village. She's the new teacher at the school and wants to live here, rather than having to drive in from Draymarket. So, we'll call her and keep our fingers crossed that she's still looking," said Hannah. Laura quickly realised their prospective tenant must be Miss Alicia Wiltshire, who was now teaching the reception class.

Then a curious thing happened, perhaps fuelled by her excitement, as another thought popped into her head and before she knew it, she'd come right out with it. "I don't suppose you need any assistance here? I don't know anything about estate agency, but I was a bank cashier for seven years and I'm good with people." Hannah said she might have enquired at a most opportune moment because they'd just opened a new branch in Draymarket and the boss could well be glad of some more assistance, so she'd ask. Laura left the office, excited at the prospect of being able to drop the kids off at school and then work part time for Randall's. It was not until he was driving into work on the Wednesday morning that Royston's thoughts again returned to the question of contacting the young woman who'd come to his rescue, but just how was he to do it? He mulled the question over for a few minutes before coming up with the idea of placing a small advert in the Gazette. When he arrived at the office, Hannah told him how the Jameson's were now looking to rent out their home following their pending move to Albany House and that Miss Alicia Wiltshire, who was luckily still looking for a place, was dropping in after school tomorrow. She also mentioned that Laura was looking for a part-time job and Royston agreed she should come in for an interview. Boss and his accident, the forthcoming merger and the prospect of a little matchmaking for him with Miss Alicia Wiltshire had been the main topics of Hannah and Heather's conversation over supper the previous evening, when they'd both imbibed more white wine than was good for them. If Royston wasn't around when she came in to arrange a viewing, they'd certainly make sure he did the show around.

Royston waited until Hannah had popped out to meet a new client before calling up the Gazette and placing a small box ad appealing for the lady who'd come to his aid in Little Oreford Lane on that fateful Saturday night to get in touch. He then promptly forgot all about it as he became totally immersed in the business of the day. Sam called saying the new Draycott housing development people were seeking a marketing strategy meeting and then he became involved in a cycle of calls to solicitors acting for vendor and purchaser in a sale that had started to run off the rails.

His mobile rang just as he was winding up his final call and he glanced at the number which came up 'Gazette Office.' That was not at all unusual because they were always calling Kim, the lady who handled all the paper's ads, but the woman who responded was not Kim, but Jackie Benson, the paper's rather pushy chief reporter, who was always after him and John Gibbs for property stories. Their working relationship was pleasant enough, but there was an edge to her that rather grated with Royston, especially as it seemed to him that she was on far better terms with John. "And what can I do for you today, Jackie?" he asked politely, but the answer to his question was not the one about some aspect of the property market, he'd expected. "Someone in the office brought your small ad to our attention and we're naturally curious to know how a mystery woman came to your aid in Little Oreford Lane." Blast! That damn woman was up to her tricks again. Even when the market was doing really well, she was always looking for a downside when writing her property features. Nothing ever seemed to be rosy in her garden and even if she'd got a garden, he bet it would be totally neglected so busy was she digging up the dirt and prying into other people's business. "That's easily explained. I had a spot of bother with my car and she came to my rescue," he said, trying to brush it all off lightly. "What sort of bother, Royston?" It was clear she wasn't going to give up so he might as well tell her the whole story, otherwise she'd only call up her contacts in the local police and fire service and find out anyway. "What a nasty experience; no wonder you'd like to thank this lady so, why don't we help by taking a picture of you at the crash scene and putting your 'Appeal for Mystery Woman' story in the paper, which is far more likely to be seen than your little box ad?" That was definitely not a good idea because the first thing people would think was that he'd been driving too fast, which was true, and had been drinking and was over the limit, which was definitely not true. "Look Jackie, I really appreciate that you'd like to help, but I think I'll just stick to my ad if you don't mind." He knew she would mind, she'd mind a lot, but he was going to stick to his guns and he didn't think she'd push it because it was a relatively small community and they'd have to go on working together.

"There is another matter I wanted to ask you about." Hell! Now what was coming? he wondered.

"We've heard you might be merging with Gibbs and Sons and we're wondering if there was any truth in it. I've tried getting in touch with John, but he doesn't seem to be around at the moment." Now Royston was in a corner and he knew it, but again, there was really no point in denying the merger plans.

"It's true, John and I have discussed the possibility, but it's got no further than that, so the last thing we'd want is anything in the paper, which might upset our staff, especially if nothing comes of it." Now it was Jackie who was in the corner. "OK, but no doubt you'll let me know if you do decide to go ahead?" Royston promised she'd be among the first to know.

Chapter 10

Was this really the time to raise his proposal for reducing his working week to three and a half days? Ben asked himself as he drove into work the following Monday morning. Laura had popped into Randall's for her prospective job chat the previous afternoon and, much to her surprise, had promptly been taken on. She was to work four days a week from 9.30am until 3pm for a trial three months, during term times. Laura's having to go back to work was no longer worrying Ben because it was clear she was excited at the prospect. So her earnings and the cash they were going to save by renting out their house would be just about enough to compensate for his reduced salary, if indeed the hospital's managing board agreed to his plan? He'd put in a formal request before close of play, hinting that if they turned him down, he'd consider his position, but what if they called his bluff? 'Oh, to hell with it. I don't care if they do, because I'll leave anyway,' Ben resolved. As it turned out, the governing board took the view that Ben Jameson was too valuable an asset to lose and agreed to his reducing his working week to three and a half days and to employing a new full-time administrative assistant in his department. They privately agreed they owed him that much because, thanks in a large part to his meticulous attention to record keeping, a potentially costly compensation claim had been avoided. Chloe, his new assistant, proved to be super efficient, so much so, that Ben actually started enjoying his job again.

Fortune also smiled on the Jameson's and Robin and Margo because they managed to employ the immediate services of a local building firm, who had their own plumbing, heating and electrical contractors, with just one phone call. The firm, it seemed, had been seriously let down by the eleventh-hour cancellation of a contract the previous day, so all the renovation work on Albany House was now in progress.

Robin and Margo were on site all week and Ben drove up to Little Oreford to help out on Thursday afternoon's and Friday's until the start of the summer holidays. Laura was now totally absorbed in her new job, but they all drove up to the house most afternoons after school to liaise with the builders and to help out in any way they could, often staying for tea with Robin and Margo. Luke and Lottie ran wild although being under strict instructions to keep within the boundaries of the property. They were having the time of their lives and so reminded Robin and Margo of their happy childhood growing up in the village.

But there was one incident that cast a small shadow over those sunlit afternoons. It happened when Laura called the children back to the house for a teatime snack. "Mum, a funny thing happened just now," said Lottie, her mouth full of chocolate spread sandwich. "We were playing close to the woods when we saw this lady looking at us through a gap in the hedge and the funny thing was, she looked just like you, Mum." Laura felt an uneasiness stealing over her. There was that striking likeness between her and the Little Oreford rector's wife and that earlier incident in The Allway Centre and now this.

It was as if something was going on in some parallel universe and it unsettled her. "There's a public footpath running through the woods and that gap where people can look into the garden, so we'll ask daddy and uncle Robin to put up a barrier so they can't see in anymore," she promised, pushing any more unsettling thoughts to the back of her mind.

As the Jameson's now had a target moving in day some three weeks ahead, it was time to secure a tenant for the Cherry Grove property and the appointment with Alicia

Wiltshire had been booked for Royston because, for one reason or another, neither Heather nor Hannah were available. Their instincts had been right because Royston did fancy Alicia Wiltshire and had even started fantasising about her at odd moments, but telling himself he was being ridiculous. For an estate agent to come on to a single woman he happened to be showing around a property was fraught with danger and he knew he would never put himself in that compromising position.

He was waiting at the front door, folder in hand, as was his custom, when a car came slowly into the close and stopped outside. As it happened, Alicia also sensed that the estate agent she'd first encountered when she'd popped into Randall's, found her attractive and she'd noticed he wasn't wearing a wedding ring, although that didn't seem to count for much nowadays. Alicia had not had anyone permanent in her life for quite a while and the few friends she did have were back home in Somerset.

But she was one of those people who possessed the rare gift of being quite at ease in her own company, loved good books and listening to classical music, so never really went out of her way to find a man. If one happened to come along to whom she felt in some way attracted, then she'd probably give it a go, but she was not really that bothered one way or the other.

Royston watched as she climbed out of her small saloon car and came towards him with a slight smile on her face. Yes, he did find her attractive; he couldn't think why, he just did. They exchanged pleasantries on the doorstep with Royston hoping she'd not had to drive far, seeing that it was in the middle of the summer holidays. She assured him it had not been a problem, but did not elaborate.

"To be honest with you, rented properties in Hampton Green are at a premium and because we knew you were looking for somewhere, we've contacted you first and have not yet released the details onto the market," he explained, as she followed him into the hall and from there into the living room. "That was very good of you," she replied, but thinking this was just salesman's patter seeing the 'For Rent' board was already up.

Alicia said little as she followed Royston from room to room, quietly recognising the two children whose faces smiled back at her from family photo frames. Yes, there was a happy family living in this house. When the tour was over, they returned to the living room and stood together side by side looking out into the small rear garden from the large double-glazed patio window.

He could smell just a hint of her perfume. Her voice was soft and he found that hugely attractive. "The rent is a little more than I wanted to pay, but if such properties are at a premium, as you say, then I guess I shall have to go for it."

Royston stood and watched admiringly as she drove away before strolling to his car opening the boot and taking out a 'Let' sign which he hung on a hook at the bottom of his board.

Three days before Laura and Ben were due to move into Albany House and about midway through the summer holidays, the weather turned wet with a series of storms blowing in from the Atlantic and across the South West of the country bringing prolonged spells of drizzle. It was what gardeners had been praying for after days of mostly warm dry weather, but it was definitely not what Laura and Ben had wanted. Up until then, all the preparations for the move had gone better than they could possibly have hoped for, even to the point where a couple of skilled painters and decorators had managed to wallpaper most of the rooms.

It also turned out that one of their wives worked in the offices at the local sale and auction rooms and was only too keen to help Laura and Ben pick up a large amount of suitable brown wood wardrobes and other furniture for a song, because it was now totally out of fashion.

Drawing back the curtains on their chosen Friday moving morning, Laura's heart sank because it was still raining. She'd been hoping against hope the weather would magically improve overnight, but of course, it had not. They all had breakfast in a haze of pent-up excitement and some trepidation over all that was to happen that day. Luke and Lottie had long given up their campaign to be allowed to be involved and Laura took them off to Sarah's with only token protests.

As they were letting the house furnished, Ben now began loading all their personal possessions into the white transit van he'd hired the previous afternoon. Laura was soon back to help.

"Goodbye, house. I wonder if we'll ever be living in you again," she said as they drove out of Cherry Grove and on the road to their new life. Luckily the rain stopped and the sun was just emerging from behind leaden clouds when they drove into Little Oreford.

Now after three months of intensive effort by the builders, Ben and Laura and Margo and Robin and their new friends, accumulated during the race to decorate and complete the furnishing, Albany House was all ready and waiting their arrival. "So this is it," said Ben as they drove down the drive and parked outside the new roof tiled entrance porch, a late edition suggested by their helpful builders. Surprisingly, there was no sign of Margo and Robin, whom they'd assumed would be there waiting to welcome them.

"Despite all the work, I still can't believe this is all really happening," said Laura, as they climbed down from the van and walked to the front door. "You do know this is my absolute dream come true, don't you?" Ben said he never would have guessed, but as he reached out to take her hand, some instinct made him glance back towards the open gate to see an angry plume of blue smoke shooting skyward in the middle distance.

"If that's a bonfire, it's a bloody big one," he remarked as Laura also looked round. "Oh my God, that looks like a house on fire!" They dropped hands, hurried back along the drive and out onto the green. Smoke, now infused with licking flames, was billowing out of a third-floor window of the mill house, behind tall gates at the far end of the green and right next to the lane leading into Little Oreford. Laura put her hand to her mouth, realising with a strange clarity that her mobile phone for raising the alarm was in her bag in the van, but Ben was already racing across the green to Margo and Robin's. His frantic banging brought an almost instant response from the couple, who had been in the hallway slipping on coats and preparing to walk across to Albany House with a bottle of bubbly and four glasses. Robin grabbed the phone from the hall stand and began dialling the emergency services, while Margo came out into the road. "Will there be anyone in there?" Laura asked breathlessly, having chased after Ben across the green, because on all her visits to the hamlet she'd never seen any sign of life coming from the big house. "I don't think so because the place has been empty, for years," shouted Margo as they started hurrying across the green towards the house with Ben already way out in front. "Is there any other way in?" he yelled, looking wildly around at Margo, having realised there were no handles on the stout wooded gates, which were far too high to climb. "Yes, there's another big wooden gate, but it's almost certain to be locked, so we'd better get our ladder," she cried, as the angry crackling sound from the fire suddenly grew louder and an acrid smell filled the air. Ben started running back across the green towards Robin, who had now emerged, but quickly turned, on shouted instructions and raced for their side gate. Minutes later, they'd thrown the ladder against the front gates and Ben had scrambled to the top. "Be careful!" yelled Laura, but before she could say another word, he was over the top and lost from view. "Ben," she screamed, now in a complete panic, but seconds later they heard a bolt being drawn back and he emerged, having pushed one of the heavy gates open. Seconds later, the sound of an explosion and shattering glass drove them all back and they turned to see the large front door, some thirty feet away across a weed covered drive, opened and two youngish men staggered out. "Oh my God," Laura uttered as, instinctively, Ben and Robin ran forward, through swirls of smoke and dragged the two out onto the green, where they collapsed onto the grass coughing and spluttering. "Is there anyone else in there?" demanded Ben, an urgency in his voice, but the two just looked at him blankly.

By now, several other neighbours had reached the scene and were asking questions and offering

102

assistance. "I don't think they speak English, Robin," Ben said, glancing back at the house to see that smoke and flames had reached the top floor windows. The two were now sitting up on the grass and gulping down glasses of water provided by one of the neighbours. "Is there anyone else in the house?" Ben asked again, but this time a little more sharply as the first sounds of a distant siren punched the air. With that, one of the two scrambled to his feet, dropping the glass as he did so, and ran off across the green making for the footpath beside Albany House.

In an instant his friend was chasing after him.

Taken completely by surprise, everyone just stood and watched them disappear from view beyond the end of the green, as a nearby patrolling police car, burst onto the scene.

Chapter 11

Jackie Benson revelled in her role as chief reporter of the Draymarket Gazette, even though there were only two other full timers, the editor, Bill Manning, and reporter cum sub-editor, Jock Murray, both experienced hacks, now in their sixties, and Ollie, a journalism student on work experience.

She enjoyed her more relaxed Friday mornings in the office above the chemist shop in High Street, because their paper had just come out and both Bill and Jock would not be in until later. She didn't really need to be there, but she was a forty-year-old with little else to do except being married to her work.

She happened to be looking down onto the street from one of the old wooden sash windows, brutes to open in the summer, when the phone rang. "Jackie, it's Jimmy down at the station. We've just sent out on a 'shout' to what sounds like a big house fire up at Little Oreford." Thanking him, she slammed down the phone, and grabbing her car keys from her desk, hurried down the dusty back stairs and out into the car park.

Jimmy really was a treasure, she thought as she manoeuvred her now battered office car out into the morning traffic and then cursed as the town's only set of traffic lights turned red against her. Once past the lights, she glanced down at her petrol gauge to see it was on empty. "Blast." The filling station was at the other end of town, so she'd have to turn around and go back through those damn lights again. "I can't believe this is happening!" she muttered.

The result was that it was another ten frustrating minutes before she'd filled up and was on her way again, this time on the longer way around, via Hampton Green, because there was no way she was going back through those damn lights again.

Back at the station, Jimmy Jones, part-time fire fighter and local plumber, who was nearly always the last one to answer a 'shout' and therefore often got left behind, was strolling back to his van. Although he would only half admit it to himself, he never actually made a real effort to be on the team, so that he could call Jackie. Most of the boys at the station disliked the pushy lady by whom they'd all been interviewed over the years for one reason or another, but not Jimmy. There was something about her he liked. He also lusted over one of the weather girls on the local news, but while she was beyond his reach, the chief reporter of the Draymarket

Gazette was not. "In your dreams, mate," had been the cruel response when he ventured to mention Jackie over a pint with a drinking pal.

By the time she reached the village, a second fire appliance from a neighbouring retained station, had arrived at the now chaotic scene. Pulling up further along the green, now thronged with local people, she grabbed her phone and notebook and climbed out of her car, immediately smelling a slight acridness in the air. Smoke was still drifting lazily from the upper windows of the mill house, but the fire now seemed to be well under control. Climbing over the temporary rope cordon thrown up along the edge of the green, she started taking pictures of the now blackened building and of the small crowd of onlookers, before hurrying over to the police car, its blue lights still flashing.

"Morning, Jackie. You're going to love this one," greeted the officer amiably as he came off the phone to the police control room. "Why's that then, Andrew?" She'd known this particular officer for several years and he was one of the more helpful ones. "It seems to be something more than a normal house fire because the locals managed to open the big front gates and drag two youngish men to safety, but as soon as they'd recovered, they scarpered. We've got their descriptions and have put out an all points alert for them." Jackie thanked him for the info and wondered where she might find those locals who'd come to the rescue. "Funnily enough, they're in the middle of moving into that place over there, so I guess that's where you'll find them," he said, nodding in the direction of Albany House.

On her way across the green, Jackie stopped to speak to several onlookers, still standing around and savouring the excitement, because nothing much ever happened in sleepy Little Oreford. She took down brief quotes from them and asked if they knew who occupied the mill house, but no one, it seemed, had a clue as to who was living there. "The place has been empty for years so those two young men were probably squatters who started the fire by accident," one elderly lady suggested. Standing a little apart from the other residents was a young woman with short cropped dark hair, who Jackie took to be in her mid-thirties as she approached her. "Hi I'm Jackie from the Gazette. Were you around when the fire started?" she asked in her most friendly manner.

It was clear in an instant that the woman had in some way been surprised by the sudden approach.

"No, I'm not from around here and I didn't see anything," she said turning and walking away.

The unexpected rebuff took Jackie by surprise, but she brushed it aside as she made her way down the drive of Albany House, around the big white van parked outside the open front door and stopped.

Hearing voices, she stepped into the impressive Victorian hallway. "Anybody home?" she called out, walking forward into the large kitchen. There she found two couples nursing mugs of coffee and surrounded by a clutter of cardboard boxes.

"Looks like you're moving in," she said, stating the obvious and introducing herself.

Laura, Ben. Robin and Margo were still on a high from all the excitement of the fire and now the moving in operation, so they happily told the Gazette's chief reporter all they knew. They willingly agreed to walk back across the green and have their pictures taken with Robin's ladder.

"No harm in being on friendly terms with the local press when it comes to our plans to reopen the inn," he suggested, tongue in cheek, when she'd gone.

"Perhaps you might also acquire the mill house seeing it's been fire damaged," replied Ben. "Now that is an idea," said Robin, shooting a sideways glance at Margo, who chose to ignore both throw away suggestions about future acquisitions.

Around two o'clock, the four strolled over to Margo and Robin's for a snack lunch, which she'd prepared earlier. "There's an awful lot of activity going on over there, even though those two might have been arsonists," said Ben, noticing there were now three police vehicles around the scene. They deviated their course across the green and approached the roped off area. "You're right, Ben, something's definitely going on," said Margo, taking in the police vehicles and what looked like an unmarked police car.

They were just turning away when they were called back and approached by the uniformed officer, who'd spoken briefly to them earlier. He was followed by a colleague in plain clothes, who introducing, himself as Detective Chief Inspector John Roberts, asked if he might call by later.

It was agreed he'd give them time to have their lunch and come over to Albany House in about forty minutes, after which his mobile sprang into life and he made his excuses and walked slowly away.

"What on earth's a detective chief inspector doing at a house fire, unless they've found a body inside or something like that?" Robin speculated over lunch. They'd only just finished when they heard him calling out from the front door which they'd left open.

There really was little more they could add to their story, but the detective took a real interest in the fact that neither of the fugitives appeared to speak English.

"Look, what's this really all about?" Robin suddenly asked, when the interview seemed to be winding up. "I wouldn't have thought that, even if those two were arsonists, it would be serious enough to warrant the appearance of a detective chief inspector."

It was clear he'd caught the detective slightly off his guard, as he was now the one being questioned. He hesitated for a moment, as if weighing up his options.

"OK, what's going on, as you so aptly put it, will be common knowledge in a couple of days, so I'm prepared to take you into my confidence as long as it stays that way." They all nodded in agreement. "Carry on, Detective Chief Inspector, because I can assure you nothing will be said by any of us, will it?" he said, turning to the others who could never have dreamt what was to come next.

"OK, it turns out that this house, right in the middle of your small community, has been used for highly illegal cannabis, or marijuana, production for what appears to have been quite some time and the two men you rescued are now being sought in connection with the crime. They clearly serviced their enterprise in the early hours via a back gate leading onto a track and down to the road, which is probably why people living around here never got suspicious." Margo agreed that she'd walked past that gate dozens of times and had never seen anything suspicious going on. "Yes, but not in the middle of the night," Robin reminded her. "So, what's going to happen now?" Ben asked.

"We'll be keeping this all to ourselves for a couple more days while the forensic team complete their work and then we'll be issuing a statement to the press. If we'd caught those jokers on site, then we might have detained them and kept the place under surveillance for a while to see who else turned up because this was far bigger than just a two-man operation, but it's too late for that now."

Laura said she'd show him out, but when they reached the front door, she asked what would happen to the two if they were caught. "That'll depend on what they have to

111

tell us, Mrs Jameson." But Laura didn't want to leave it there.

The overall impression she'd gained during the few brief minutes before they ran off was that they were both scared and vulnerable and her heart had gone out to them. "There's been a lot in the papers recently about people sneaking into the country illegally and then being lured into slave labour. Do you think these two might fall into that category?" she pressed. "That's certainly a possibility," he conceded.

Later that afternoon, Sarah arrived with Luke and Lottie and her own children, who were soon playing together in the garden having run all over the house in high excitement, bouncing on the beds in Luke and Lottie's new bedrooms.

"Thank God for a bit of normality," said Ben as he stood watching them play.

When Alicia Wiltshire popped into Randall's on the Sunday morning to pick up the keys to her new rented home in Cherry Grove, Royston happened to be on his own. Giving her a broad smile, he got up from his desk and went over to the cabinet where rental property and other keys were kept.

"I hope you'll be very happy there," he said without looking around.

Studying his broad shoulders and slim, smartly suited back, she was not displeased. 'Why shouldn't she have a little fling with this clearly unattached, well-dressed and friendly chap, whom she judged to be around her own age?' she asked herself.

Alicia gave him a gentle smile as he returned to the desk. "Please, take a seat while we complete the paperwork and just have a final run over the tenancy agreement," he invited.

Alicia did as she was bid.

She was wearing a pair of slightly worn dark trousers, a white blouse and an elderly green sweater and was obviously in moving in mode.

"There's no need to go over the agreement. I've already checked it and all is in order," she said, producing her signed copy from the folder she'd already placed on the desk in front of her. Royston smiled back. "I don't suppose you need me to arrange some help, with moving in?" he inquired.

"No, I'll be fine, but I expect I'll be in need of a large glass of chilled white wine by the time I've finished."

There was a pause as Royston internalised what seemed like a clear 'come on' signal or was it? "I'm not sure the Jameson's will have left any in their fridge," he said smiling. There was another agonising pause as Alicia returned his smile, but made no immediate response. He hesitated. "Well perhaps I could bring a chilled bottle around or buy you a drink at The Lion later on this evening?" he suggested. There was another pause while she considered the invitation. "Yes, a drink at The Lion would be nice," she replied. Alicia had hardly left the office when the phone rang. "Is that Royston Randall?" It was a young woman's voice. "That's right, but if you're selling something I'm not interested," he replied sharply. "No, I'm not selling anything, Mr Randall, I'm simply responding to your advert in the Draymarket Gazette. It took a moment for the penny to drop. "Oh yes, of course! You're the lady who came to my rescue and I wanted to thank you personally," he explained. "So I'm free tomorrow night, if you are!" came the instant response and before he'd had time to think about it properly, he'd arranged to meet Tanya Talbot in Bradley's, the new wine bar in Draymarket High Street.

"You'll recognise me easily enough because I have very short blonde hair and I'll be wearing a dark green fitted jacket, black trousers and black boots." Royston said he'd be in a light-coloured suit as he'd be coming straight from his office, also in High Street, but before he could say more, she'd ended the call, leaving him feeling a little uncomfortable at the thought of his whirlwind impromptu date.

By the time he got home, he'd made up his mind to call and put her off, at least for a couple of weeks until he saw how things were working out with Alicia, but when he checked his call log, she'd withheld her number. That settled it. He'd have to meet up with Tanya, if only for a quick drink. 'Talk about busses all coming along at once!'

It was quiet in The Lion that Sunday evening. Royston had flipped over the 'closed' sign on his office door forty minutes early so that he could give himself a little more time to nip home, shower and change into something more casual.

Entering The Lion, Royston, looked around, but Alicia had not arrived and there was a relief crew behind the bar, which meant that Geoff and Pat were having a night off. Then an uncomfortable thought occurred to him. "I

take it you are doing food tonight," he asked anxiously.
Thankfully everything was on and the specials were on
the board. Armed with a large glass of Sauvignon Blanc,
he settled himself in an alcove from where he could
watch the door while studying the menu and the
specials.

Time ticked anxiously by and Royston was almost
through his glass of wine when Alicia suddenly
appeared, still in her work clothes. "I'm most terribly
sorry. There was loads more to do than I'd imagined and
I simply didn't keep my eye on the time.

Look at me still in my old togs and you looking so smart."
Royston told her not to worry because it was chill-out
time and he'd go to the bar to get her the promised large
glass of white wine. "Will the Sauvignon Blanc be OK?"
She nodded, sitting down and picking up the menu
because she'd not stopped for lunch and was famished.
"I hope the Jameson's left the house in a tidy state," he
said, after rejoining her and quietly savouring her
physical presence. It was such a long time since he'd
been so close to a woman, whose soft voice alone was
really exciting him. "Oh yes. The house was immaculate
and Mrs Jameson had even left a few essential
provisions like milk, bread and some eggs and there was

116

a vase of fresh flowers on the kitchen table." Alicia again apologised for not being on time. "I'm rather a stickler for having things how I like them. So I moved some of the furniture around and then changed the layout again until I was happy with it all," she explained,

"Then I had all my things to put away and my large collection of books to sort through and so it went on until I looked up and saw the time."

Alicia had eaten at The Lion several times with colleagues from the school so she chose the duck, which she said had been particularly good the last time she was in. Royston said he'd have that too. "Now do tell me all about yourself," she said giving him her lovely gentle smile "OK, I'll go first, but it's going to be your turn afterwards," he said as they clinked glasses and Alicia noted that his was only a small glass. "That's because I have to drive home while you only have to walk around the corner and seeing that I've already had one, even this small one may be too much." Alicia was sure he'd be OK after they'd eaten and chatted for a bit, but now she wanted to hear all about him. "There's not really much to tell. I grew up and went to school hereabouts, took a history degree, because I thought I might teach. But my dad's health started failing so I came home to help him

117

with the family estate agency business, then he died and I took over and the rest, as they say is history," he explained.

Did he ever regret that it was circumstance that had chosen his career path, she wondered? "Not really, because I enjoy the work and never wake up on a Monday morning not wanting to go in, but I guess, everyone's path through life is subject to their reaction to circumstances," he replied.

"Goodness me! This conversation could start getting pretty deep, so maybe we should save it for another time when we're not having our getting to know more about you session," she suggested.

So, there might well be another time and that thought excited Royston. He also liked the way she said 'goodness me.'

"OK, so if we are returning to the subject of getting to know you, then I guess it's your turn," he invited.

Alicia liked his easy manner and how naturally they were just chatting away together, so perhaps she had found her new man. "I was born in Somerset, the youngest of three sisters by some eleven years, so definitely not planned, although my parents persisted in denying that. My father worked on big civil engineering projects around the world. He was often away for months at a time and my mother used to go with him in later years when my sisters were away at university. As a result, I spent a lot of time living with my aunt, who was really the one who brought me up."

That all sounded a bit harsh, said Royston. "Well, no, actually it wasn't because her daughter, Cat, my cousin, was around my age and we got on famously. We both loved tennis and running and belonged to a local athletics club where we happily competed against one another." Was she still into running? Royston asked. "I certainly am and I play tennis whenever I get the chance," she replied

"Being an estate agent isn't the most active of occupations and I know I should take more exercise, but I never seem to get around to it," Royston admitted. He wondered why she had never become a physical education teacher. "Actually, I did think quite seriously about that, but came to the conclusion that if it was my job, then I wouldn't enjoy sport nearly as much in my leisure time, she explained. "So what do you do in your spare time Royston?" she asked. He told her about his being the secretary of the regional motoring club and owning a vintage sports car which was under repair

119

because he'd been in a scrape with it. luckily, she didn't question him further. "Maybe we could go out for a drive when it's back on the road." he ventured. It was almost as bad as inviting a girl home to see one's etchings and he immediately regretted making the suggestion, but Alicia said she'd look forward to that.

She told him how she'd gone to teacher training college and had taken a number of primary school positions around the country before alighting on Hampton Green. "I'd always worked in towns before, but something about the advert for your village school appealed to me so here I am." They parted an hour later, having agreed to meet up for supper again at The Lion the day after tomorrow. Life certainly seemed to be picking up, Royston thought as he drove home. Alicia was also deep in thought as she strolled along the High Street, past Randall's estate agency and around the corner into Cherry Grove. 'He certainly seemed to be a nice chap, but it was interesting how we'd both, probably subconsciously, kept off the subject of past relationships,' she thought.

Chapter 12

Royston started his day by calling in at the Hampton
Green office on his way to open up in Draymarket.
Heather and Hannah already had their heads down,
coping with all the new Greenfield Park enquiries which
had started flooding in since the 'Executive Homes
Coming Soon' boards had gone up along the boundary
of the new development on the edge of the market town.
Laura was rapidly getting to grips with her new role and
was already proving her value to the fast-expanding
agency operation. "Coffee, Boss," she greeted him as he
came through the door.' This 'boss' business would
have to be contained to the present company only, after
they'd absorbed the Gibbs' team, Royston decided.
It was while she was making Royston's coffee, that the
frightened look, on the younger of the two men's faces
as he scrambled to his feet, popped back into her mind,
as it had done on several earlier occasions.
It had been arranged that Royston would meet John
Gibbs in his office to complete the merger, which now
included one important amendment in that the business
would trade as Royston Randall and not as Randall and
Gibbs. John had wanted to keep his name above the

door, but eventually agreed that if he was to be a silent partner with no active involvement, other than receiving his monthly remuneration, then there was actually, little point in there being joint names above the door.

In what seemed like no time at all, Royston was locking up and strolling on a cloud of elation the few steps down the High Street to Bradley's to meet Tanya Talbot.

To his surprise, she turned out to be everything that Alicia was not and her effect on him was little short of electric.

She was slim, vivacious, and attentive and three hours, two bottles of an expensive red wine and several plates of tapas later they'd exchanged life stories and were making their way up the stairs to her flat, which just happened to be almost opposite. Royston's capacity for drinking wine and staying reasonably sober was expansive, but his experience of 'shorts' was not, with the result that four exotic cocktails later, all generously mixed by Tanya from her own mini bar of spirits, he was drunk.

Shortly afterwards, they were leaving a trail of discarded clothes as they staggered into her large and expensively decorated and furnished bedroom and collapsing onto her bed, where Royston landed on top of her and pushing against just a little soft resistance, exploded and quickly passed out.

Light was flooding the room through voile curtains when he became conscious and pushed himself slowly up onto one shoulder to see Tanya coming slowly towards him carrying two mugs. She was wearing his now slightly crumpled cream office shirt, her small, pert breasts just making their soft presence known. It was open at the front, revealing her belly button and small blond forest. "I thought strong coffee might be in order," she announced with a smile. Royston dragged his tired eyes around to the bedside cabinet, where a small clock told him it was now 9.40am and meant he should already be at his desk in Hampton Green!

"Now, what would you like to do today?" she asked, placing a steaming mug on a silver coaster next to the clock.

Royston's heart began thumping in panic as the reality of the past fourteen hours suddenly hit him like a sledgehammer and his thoughts switched cruelly to his date with Alicia that evening!

"Look, I'm awfully sorry, but I've got a busy day of appointments ahead and I should have been in my office thirty minutes ago," he replied, now brushing a hand through his hair. "Oh dear, and I'm wearing your shirt, but never mind, I'll whip it off and iron it in a jiffy," she said, treating him to a disappearing view of her nubile naked body. "I can't have my man going to work in a crumpled shirt," she called back as she disappeared into the living room. "Oh Christ. This is all moving far too fast", muttered Royston who now felt helpless and totally out of control of the situation.

He climbed out of bed, retrieved his boxer shorts, which were luckily on the carpet close by, and went in search of the rest of his clothes.

He entered the living room where Tanya, now wearing a bath robe, had already put up her ironing board and was going to work on his shirt. "So, shall we go out again tonight, darling?" Her suggestion threw Royston into renewed panic.

Was this really happening, or was he in the middle of some nightmare prompted by his yearning for some close female company?

He hesitated, wondering for a split second if she should call Alicia and cry off on the date he was really looking forward to.

No, the thought of another wham bam evening with this pushy young woman, who'd already made up her mind that they were in a relationship, would be all too much for him.

"Look Tanya, I really can't make tonight because I'm secretary of our local motoring club and we have a special meeting which I just can't get out of."

Tanya said that was quite all right and she'd come with him if that was OK. Now Royston was well and truly cornered and stone cold sober.

"Look, Tanya," he said again, "Just because we've spent one night together, you really can't assume we're now in a relationship because that's not how it works."

She stopped ironing and was gazing at him with her pretty face now a mask of stone, but she'd left the hot iron on his expensive shirt where, within seconds, it was beginning to scorch.

"And I thought you were an honourable man. Too bad about the shirt," she said, pulling it off the ironing board and tossing it at him. "I think you'd better go, don't you?"

Royston needed no second bidding, bending to retrieve his trousers from the living room floor and climbing into them. It took a couple more minutes to find and put on his shoes and then grabbing his jacket, which he'd left draped over a chair, he hurriedly donned it.

"I hope we can still be friends," he said as he opened her heavy front door and escaped into the hallway, but no words followed his hasty retreat from the scene. Luckily, her apartment also had a rear access and he managed to hurry up the lane running along the back of High Street and make it to the safety of his car without being seen.

Hannah, who was holding the fort at Hampton Green for the day, was just beginning to wonder what had happened to him when he called to apologise for not being in touch earlier and to explain he was not feeling too well.

"It's OK, Boss. It's still quiet here, but Heather and I spent quite a lot of time last night thinking about the merger and we've also come up with a couple of ideas, should you want to expand still further at some point in the future."

Royston said he'd always appreciated their enthusiasm and would be very keen to consider what they had in mind, once things had settled down, but if she could manage on her own for the rest of the day, that would be helpful.

Driving home, he dived straight in the shower, ignoring for once, the winking red 'message received' light on his phone, but when he emerged and pressed the play button, Alicia's soft voice filled the room. She was awfully sorry, but she'd developed a nasty cough and cold so could she possibly cry off tonight and in return perhaps he'd like to come around to her for supper around seven the following Saturday?

Heart sinking, he called her back and when she didn't answer, left a message saying he was sorry she wasn't well, but would be delighted to accept her invitation. He'd only just put down the phone when a text arrived on his mobile.

'Dear Royston. I'm really sorry I ruined your lovely shirt. It was completely out of order. I guess I was just disappointed that I wouldn't be seeing you again after we'd got on so well and had such a lovely time. My trouble is that I'm terribly headstrong, I always have been and just jump to conclusions when I have no right to. Can you forgive me? Tanya xxx.'

Royston sat down at his kitchen table now beginning to feel guilty that he hadn't been able to get out of her apartment fast enough, when all she'd done was to make him a mug of coffee and suggested they should spend the day together, so now what was he going to do?

Chapter 13

News that the old mill house in Little Oreford had been used for growing cannabis broke on local radio early on the following Monday morning. It was followed by a police press conference, including a public appeal for information and the news that two suspects had already been detained. But what was not been revealed at the time was that a substantial stash of much harder drugs, including cocaine, had been found at the scene.

Less than two hours later, the rural peace of the village was shattered by the arrival of a media posse, including local TV and radio reporters, the regional news agency and Jackie Benson from the Gazette, fuming that none of her local police contacts had tipped her off in advance.

All those at home around the green were pestered for interviews. Robin and Margo had decided to keep quiet about their part in the rescue, but that was not to be, because a neighbour told of their involvement and Robin agreed, after much pressing, to stand in front of the cameras and then to be interviewed for radio. Jackie, still feeling aggrieved, stood back and took a series of picture on her phone. All this was going to be old news by Friday, her publication day, so what she needed was an 'exclusive' throwing some new light on the scene and then all these hacks would be chasing around after her, but finding that angle was going to be easier said than done.

Laura, Ben and the children watched it all on the local evening news with the kids becoming particularly excited when Uncle Robin's face suddenly appeared on their new wide screen TV.

Later, when they were in bed, Laura returned to the subject of the two young cannabis growers, now in custody, and wondered if they were from Eastern European countries, which had joined the EU, and were in fact modern day slaves. "If you're right, and we don't know that, why are you so interested, darling?" Laura felt her face colouring. "They just seemed so vulnerable, although we only saw them for a few minutes. But if they had been held against their will and kept prisoners for all that time simply out of fear, then they're going to need support when they're released."

Now she'd revealed what she'd been pushing around in her mind for the last couple of days. Ben hesitated over how he should respond. Up until quite recently, his reaction would have been to suggest that maybe her

129

work at Randall's, plus looking after the kids and their much bigger house should have been quite enough of a challenge without becoming involved in the life of two cannabis growers, but that was the old Ben.

Since being allowed to escape from his highly stressful job on Thursdays and Fridays, meaning he now had four days off in a row to recharge his batteries, he was generally in a far more relaxed frame of mind. "If you want to get involved, darling, then I guess you should." His reaction took her slightly by surprise. "That's settled then. First thing tomorrow morning, I'll call that detective inspector, who gave us his card. I'm sure he'll know what's happening to them." Before contacting John Roberts, Laura popped in to discuss her plan with Margo. "Of course, we should offer our help if they really are innocent," was her instant response.

Detective Chief Inspector Roberts picked up Laura and Margo's call immediately and was able to confirm, that the situation was, surprisingly, pretty much as they had supposed it might be.

The two were Polish and single and had come to the UK separately with the promise of jobs in the farming industry, as advertised on their social media back home. But it was a snare and after being taken to the old mill and surrendering their passports, they were told that growing these plants was highly illegal and if they didn't carry on with it, they'd be exposed and could expect tough prison sentences.

"But just how could they both be so gullible?" asked Laura.

Chief Inspector Roberts said that was easily explained because they were feeling alone and vulnerable when confronted by their tough captors, who were clearly highly manipulative and controlling. So what was going to happen to them now?" Laura asked. "They're being freed on Wednesday and, as they are not here illegally, they're being released into the care of Social Services. They have been found some temporary accommodation, while they apply for fresh passports and all the other documentation required if they are to stay in the UK," he explained. "So do they have any money to keep them going, at least for the time being?" she asked. At this point, the inspector, who had a steadily growing mountain of work on his desk and for whom the case on these two was now closed, became more diffident. "I really can't help you any further, so I suggest you get in touch with Social Services." Realising that she'd come to the end of her rope, she thanked him for being so helpful.

"Look, Laura, you have the children and your job to think about, so I'll do some digging and see if I can come up with the name of the case worker involved and find out if there's anything we can do to help," volunteered Margo.

As was not entirely unexpected, the extremely hard-pressed senior social services case worker, who'd suddenly found herself with two homeless 'Poles' on her hands, needed them like the proverbial hole in the head. So when Margo eventually got hold of her, Janice Evans could see no reason why two well-meaning members of the community shouldn't play a supportive role.

It was agreed that after the two had been released from custody on Wednesday and she'd accompanied them to the temporary bed and breakfast accommodation reserved for them in Draymarket, then Margo and Laura could be there to welcome them and offer their support.

"But you must understand, it will be entirely up to them to decide if they want to be helped and, if not, then you'll have done your best."

Later that afternoon, Luke and Lottie pleaded with Ben to replay last night's local news programme so they could see Uncle Robin again. As neither he nor Margo had managed to watch it the first time around, they came over as well and were to stay for supper. Before focussing on Robin, the camera showed the fire damaged mill house. It then panned around the green to pick up a young woman standing apart from the small crowd of onlookers and, although she was a little way off, there could be no mistake because it was Laura's shadowy double and the vision made her shudder. Once the children had gone off to bed, a little earlier than usual and under protest, she got Ben to rerun the programme and they all waited for the image to appear. "It's quite uncanny, but she does look a lot like you, Laura," Ben admitted and Robin and Margo couldn't help but agree. "I'm pretty certain she's the woman, I spotted briefly in the Allway Centre and must also be the one who Lottie saw standing and peering into the garden from the footpath the other afternoon. Talking of which Ben, you really must get on and put up some sort of barricade, so people can't look in." For some reason, neither Laura nor Margo had previously mentioned the strong likeness they'd discovered between Laura and the Rev Potter's wife, so Robin popped back home for the old family album to show Ben. They all agreed the likeness was undeniable, but came to the conclusion it

133

just had to be a pure coincidence? Robin brought their musings down to earth by suggesting that, as their's was a small community it, shouldn't be too difficult to find Laura's lookalike, if they ever felt they really needed to. "It's my guess we'd find her down the road in Yardley Upton, because it's an easy walk up here through the fields and that would explain why she was on the footpath that afternoon and on the green the other day and why she seems to appear and then disappear," he suggested.

When supper was over, Robin brought up the subject of his plans to acquire, restore and reopen the old coaching inn opposite and revealed that he'd manged to get in touch with the owners and it now appeared they might be amenable to selling.

"But first, we'll have to do our homework and find out if it would be possible to reopen the inn and what the reaction of our neighbours, and indeed everyone living in and around Little Oreford, would be. If reopening isn't going to be possible for one reason or another, then we could always restore the property to a high standard and trade it as an upmarket B&B, with hired staff. This could be highly lucrative and help to fund the mill restoration project, if that also went ahead," he suggested. "Robin do you really think you still have the energy for all of this?" asked Margo, who'd now realised that attempting to put the brakes on her brother's plans was really quite pointless. "Of, course I have and, if anything, it will give me a completely new lease of life and besides that I've now got Ben to help me, haven't I, Ben?"

Chapter 14

Royston wandered around his kitchen on Sunday morning, slowly making himself some breakfast and feeling disappointed that he'd not seen Alicia last night and had so rudely said 'no' to Tania having spent the previous night with her.

But did he really want to become any further involved with a clearly impetuous and pretty headstrong woman and did he really believe her almost unbelievable life story?

She had, it seemed, been given up for adoption at birth and spent her childhood in and out of foster homes.

"I was always pretty determined to have my own way, which is why I went through so many of them. Anyway, I escaped from their clutches just as soon as I could and because I'd hated school and had absolutely no qualifications, I went to work for a care agency going into people's homes and doing all the usual stuff. And do you know, I really enjoyed it. For the first time in my life people were looking up to me," she paused, gazing into Royston's sympathetic eyes. "That's because they were usually in their armchairs or in bed!" she laughed. "No, seriously, most of them were really appreciative and

136

used to look forward to my visits. The pay was rubbish, but I got together with another girl and we shared a grotty flat and did stuff in the evenings, plus the occasional pot if we weren't doing a night shift somewhere." Royston leant over to top up her glass and asked if she'd needed any qualifications. "Not really, but funnily enough, I suddenly felt motivated to get some, which I then did because I'm actually pretty quick on the uptake when I choose to be. My plan was to set up my own agency and start making shed loads of money like my bosses seemed to be. Then, right out of the blue, a most amazing thing happened. An old man I was particularly fond of because he was so mean, but had a really wicked sense of humour, suddenly popped his clogs and left me a fortune. He lived alone in a small bungalow and was so disagreeable that no one ever went near him except me.

Before I made my first visit, my agency boss told me no one ever lasted more than a few weeks, because either they walked out or he sacked them, but, somehow, we just hit it off.

One day I asked him why he always insisted we shared a single teabag when he had several packets in the cupboard and he told me he didn't believe in being wasteful. OK, I said, let's see just how many cuppas we can make from one teabag if we dry it out overnight. This game went on for several weeks until I suggested I buy a better quality tea so that we could get even more cups out of a bag. Yes, you can, but only after we've used up all the packets in the cupboard, he told me. Anyway, it turned out that he'd had been playing the stock market for years and by the time of his death he'd built up a portfolio, worth millions." She held out her glass for another top up and Royston asked how much she'd been left, although he knew it was none of his business. "To tell you the truth, I don't really know because all the cash is held in a trust, which he set up with his bank and from which I can draw up to £3,000 a month for life, but there's a codicil and that is that if I marry then I only get £500 a month."

Royston didn't know whether or not to believe her story, but it rang true in the fact that her flat was clearly expensive and she was extremely well dressed.

He wanted to know what'd she'd done then. "I did what I'd always wanted to do and that was to travel the world, not as a backpacker staying in grubby hostels and cheap hotels while taking on casual jobs, but in luxury."

Royston never did get to hear what happened to Tanya

next because by the time he'd told her his totally boring story, they'd finished another bottle of wine and had gone back to her apartment.

He decided to spend the day working on his garden, which he'd rather ignored of late, and because he didn't have his now wrecked and under repair car to wash. His thoughts kept returning to Tanya as he walked slowly up and down, mowing his lawn. He needed to reply to her text but what should he say?

All his instincts told him he could be playing with fire if he didn't close the door on the encounter right now, but he also knew he was the proverbial moth being drawn inexorably towards her flame.

All resistance brushed aside, he fished his phone out of his pocket and went and sat down on a bench. 'Dear Tanya. It's me who should be apologising to you for walking out on you like that. It's no wonder you felt upset and please don't worry about the shirt xxx!' He'd sort of expected she'd respond quite quickly and even stopped his mowing so that he wouldn't miss her reply, but no text came and now he was feeling really disappointed. Oh! how perverse was human nature. After his unexpected night with her, he couldn't get out of her apartment fast enough and now he was feeling unhappy because she hadn't answered his message. 'Get a grip Royston,' he scolded himself as he pushed the mower back into his garden shed and decided that he'd go into his office after all and do something useful rather than moping around at home.

Hannah was really pleased to see him because Heather had gone down with some bug and was not at all well and she wanted to nip home to make sure she was OK.

"Why on earth didn't you tell me that this morning when I called to say I wouldn't becoming in?" Royston scolded.

"I know, I really should have done, but I didn't want to let you down," she admitted. "Look Han, I know things have started getting rather busy around here and will probably go on doing so as we absorb the Gibbs' business, but that doesn't mean you mustn't tell me when there are personal issues we need to address."

"I know you're both committed to our business one hundred per cent, but your health and wellbeing must always come first."

"Go on home and take the rest of the day off because I'm here now." Hannah needed no second bidding to grab her coat and black leather shoulder bag and head off along the high street. Something made her look up to see that the late morning sun was now at such an angle that it was spotlighting the Red Lion's sign. Then she was remembering last New Year's Eve riotous party at the pub when she and Heather had climbed out of a balcony window and painted the animal gold for a dare. Royston spend the rest of the day half expecting a call or a text from Tania, but none came.

It was around 10am on the Wednesday morning that Laura and Margo set off on their mission of mercy to meet up with the social worker and the two young Polish men.

"Don't be tempted to bite off more than you can chew with your offers of help and support for these two chaps," Robin called after Margo as she rushed out of the door to Laura's car now drawn up outside. She stopped dead in the doorway and turned. "Robin Lloyd, I really can't believe I am hearing this coming from Mr let's buy and reopen the old inn and restore the mill himself!" Their faces fell as they pulled up outside a shabby bed and breakfast establishment on the outskirts of the town at least thirty minutes before Janice Evans was due to arrive with her just released charges. "What a horribly depressing place," said Laura, looking at the substantial stone built 1930's semi, which had clearly seen much better days and was now used mostly by the council as an interim hostel for homeless families.

It was especially shocking coming, as they had, from lovely homes in picturesque and leafy Little Oreford, cocooned from the real world.

"Surely, we can do better than this for them," Laura murmured as they sat there taking in the rusty B&B sign and the drab curtains, hanging limply from the two big bay front windows and looking like they'd never seen the inside of a washing machine. "Maybe, if they're willing, we should see if they'll come with us around to the Gazette to tell their story, which might prompt the whole community to pitch in and help," suggested Margo.

"That's a brilliant idea," said Laura.

Surprisingly, when Alek and Danek were introduced, they recognised Laura and Margo from the day of the fire, even though they'd only been with them for a few minutes.

They were all ushered into a large and shabbily furnished living room by a friendly and overweight landlady.

The two had arrived in the same clothes from the day of the fire, but had been given some essentials including soap, toothbrushes and shaving kits and these they'd brought with them in a single plastic shopping bag. Janice explained that their rent for a twin room had been paid in advance for a month, during which time they would need to make contact with the various agencies re the issuing of new passports and other documentation required. She gave them a pay-as-you-go mobile with £30 of credit, together with a printed list of the numbers of all the agencies they needed to contact.

Finally, she handed over £50 each, for which they had to sign and agree to repay should they decide to remain in the UK.

To Laura and Margo's surprise, both men spoke reasonably good English and, after some hesitation, agreed to accompany them to the Gazette where Jackie Benson came down to meet them at the front counter. Right up until that morning, she'd been faced with the problem of finding a fresh angle for the Gazette's page one lead story about the old mill house cannabis discovery. But nothing else of any significance had come up to push it further down the page. Their story was her eleventh-hour gift from the gods and, after they'd told it, she suggested they go back with her to Little Oreford, so she could get a picture of them outside the fire damaged mill house. But Alek and Danek had no desire to go anywhere near the place, or to have their pictures taken, and Laura and Margo demanded their wishes be respected, especially as they'd been so forthcoming about their ordeal.

Margo suggested that anyone in the town wishing to help support the two during their stay in Draymarket could call her.

"Sounds a great idea to me," said Jackie, now anxious to get on and write her new and quite sensational front-page story.

The town's response would make a great follow-up for next week and this gift of a story could well run on for weeks and weeks. 'Opposition eat your hearts out,' she thought as she hurried back upstairs. She'd agreed to include Margo's contact details at the end of the report, but now it occurred to her that perhaps it was the paper that should be receiving the calls and therefore in the driving seat and not Margo Lloyd.

Chapter 15

While Laura and Margo were on their mission of mercy,
Laura's friend Sarah had driven up to Little Oreford with
Oliver and Andrew to look after Luke and Lottie because
it was half term and all four were now outside playing
hide-and-seek in the garden. She had made a cup of
coffee and was sitting in the lounge window reading a
magazine while vaguely keeping an eye on them. Lottie,
with her hands over her eyes, was busily counting up to
one hundred under the bough, where the remains of the
old rope swing had been. before daddy had taken it
down.

When she'd finished and her hands had dropped from
her soft face, now flushed just a little pink with
excitement, there was that lady standing by the gate who
looked just like mummy!

"Lottie, are you coming to find us or not?" yelled Luke
from behind some bushes on the other side of the
garden.

Tanya Talbot was the last person on Royston's mind
later that afternoon when his phone rang as he headed
back to the Hampton Green office, having been in
Draymarket all day.

It was Heather calling to say that a woman, who hadn't given her name, was now waiting for him over at The Lion.

"We knew you were on your way back, so we asked her to take a seat, but she said she'd go over to the pub and wait for you there." Royston's thought process now went into overdrive.

The very last thing he wanted was to be seen in The Lion with Tanya because the pub was the village gossip factory and what if Alicia should happen to come in with a couple of her colleagues, what the hell would he do then?

It was bad enough that Hannah and Heather had found out about her and heaven knows what they might be thinking!

Pulling into a layby, he stopped the car, quickly found Tanya's number, and called it and the response came almost instantly. "Oh, darling, there you are. I guess your staff told you that I'm waiting for you in the pub, so what shall I get you?"

Royston cast wildly around for a response. "Hi, Tanya, great to hear from you, but I'm actually miles away on the far side of Yardley Upton and am not planning to come back to the office tonight, so why don't we meet at Bradley's, say at eight?"

Would she swallow the lie? He waited. "That's a shame. I came over because I wanted to surprise you, but never mind. I'll see you in the wine bar."

Royston drove home in a daze, highly relieved that he'd averted a potential disaster, but completely undecided over what to do next. He couldn't deny he was attracted to her and had actually been disappointed when she'd not replied to his text.

But now she seemed to be full on again and it was almost a foregone conclusion as to what would happen after they'd had a few drinks at Bradleys and gone back to her flat. Then he was thinking of Alicia, who'd probably already planned her menu for Saturday night and how he'd feel inside, if he turned up at her house knowing that Tanya was still on his scene.

It didn't bear thinking about and, besides that, she'd clearly want to go out again on Saturday night, so how would he talk his way out of that one? The whole situation was impossible so just what was he to do now? 'Think, Royston, think,' his father's words again echoed in his head.

Reaching home, he made a cuppa and sat at the kitchen table calmly considering his options. While clearly wealthy and seriously attractive to any man, she was also, on past performance, volatile, impetuous, and headstrong and the sort of woman who, in reality, would be here today and definitely gone tomorrow. What on earth she saw in him he couldn't imagine, so the chances of any relationship with her lasting had a snowball's chance in hell. "If I meet her at the wine bar with the full intention of explaining that she's not really my type, it'll either end in a nasty row or I'll succumb to her charms and end up in bed with her again and then what will I do?" he said aloud to himself. There was only one option, he'd have to call her right now and end it over the phone. He knew it was a cowardly way out. but he didn't trust himself to do otherwise.

She listened in silence as he explained that, while he found her very attractive, he didn't feel in his heart that their, so far brief relationship, had much chance of going anywhere because they were on such different paths. Her good fortune had made her a woman of the world, who appeared to want to keep on moving, while he was really a pretty boring country estate agent as rooted to the area as the foundation of all the houses he sold.

Royston was expecting her to slam the phone down at any moment, but to his surprise she didn't. "Don't worry, I should never have put you on the spot by suddenly tuning up at your office, having not even responded to that nice text you sent me, so let's just agree to be friends?"

In that moment Royston felt like some unfortunate kayaker trying to shake off a circling shark that was simply refusing to go away.

He wanted to put an end to their fledgling relationship, but now she was being so nice and understanding, he simply didn't have the heart to do it and found himself agreeing that they would meet up again in a couple of weeks.

A banner headline in the Draymarket Gazette marked 'exclusive' and by-lined Jackie Benson, quickly drew the town's attention on that Friday morning, to the story of the two young Polish men who'd been pressurised into growing cannabis in an old mill in the nearby hamlet of Little Oreford. The two, it was reported, had been found temporary accommodation in a local B&B, but if anyone could offer support in some way, they were welcome to get in touch with Jackie, or one of her colleagues at the paper.

By lunchtime, the Gazette had received several calls from those interested in helping Alek and Danek, but editor Bill Norton put a slight dampener on Jackie's enthusiasm by pointing out that if anyone was going to take the opposite view, then that would surely come in letters early next week.

Bill had spent over thirty years in regional morning and evening newspapers, but then escaped the constant pressures of daily deadlines by semi-retiring to Draymarket to edit the Gazette, followed shortly after by his lifelong friend and colleague Jock Harris, who came in as sub-editor in charge of production. "You've been a bit curmudgeonly over this Polish story, Bill, and it's not like you," said Jock as they sat with their lunchtime pints over at The Carpenters. "I know you're probably right, but my instincts tell me we could be sailing into troubled waters with this one, so I hope I'll be proved wrong."

A movement by the door suddenly caught Jock's attention.

"Now, she's what I call an attractive young woman," he said, looking up from his pint and following Tanya Talbot approvingly as she made her way towards the bar. "And what's more, it looks like she's got a copy of the Gazette."

Bill turned slowly in his chair, deliberately trying not to make his movements too obvious. "Jock, she could be your daughter!" That was indeed true, his friend conceded while keeping up an unwanted commentary, as the woman walked past the bar and disappeared into the toilets. He was still watching as she emerged some minutes later and made her way towards the back of the room and joined an older man.

"She's definitely a stunner, but I don't much like the look of him," he said quietly, as he took in her stocky well-dressed companion, who had an air of menace about him and looked as if he could handle himself in a rough situation. "Time to go, I think," suggested Jock, immediately averting his gaze from the man, who'd suddenly looked up in his direction.

Jackie had her sandwich in the office, as was her usual habit, and by the time they returned she'd contacted most of the people who had either emailed or left messages.

"The response has been quite amazing," she announced once they had returned to their screens. "A fruit and arable farmer over at Yardley needs two extra pickers and is offering to take them on for the rest of the summer and also to provide them with accommodation, which he says is of a quality standard. He's got several other Polish and Rumanian workers, so at least our two will be in familiar company. "I've also heard from a local builder's wife, who says her husband needs some assistance should our two boys have any painting or carpentry skills and there's been a further call from the manager of the High Street hospice shop saying Alek and Danek are welcome to drop in and choose any extra clothing they may need." Jackie called to update their social worker before popping over to Broadway Villas to deliver the good news.

Tanya sat down opposite her boss and placed the paper in front of him. He studied it for a few moments. "Now there's a gift. The authorities appear to have swallowed the slave story and have let our boys go," he said, slowly sipping his malt whisky.

"So now I can call the paper with my offer of help, find out where they are and go and pick them up," suggested Tanya.

"Yes, you could, but far better to wait until the new place you've found is ready for production and besides, the police can be such cunning bastards at times and this might well be a set-up so, no, we'll just wait and see for the moment. All you'll have to do is to keep buying this stupid little paper because next Friday it will probably tell you all you need to know about what our two are up to."

Tanya wasn't so sure that leaving the two men, wherever they were, for the time being was such a good idea because, once they'd had a taste of freedom, would they want to come back? Still if she did pick them up, then she'd have all the hassle of looking after them so she'd leave them to their own devices, as instructed.

"How are you settling in here, Tanya?" he asked. "I've found myself a nice flat and have started dating a boring local estate agent just to pass the time, but he's a frightened little rabbit and I scare him half to death, so I'm just playing a little game with him at the moment." He gave her a knowing look. "OK, but I'll not be happy if we have to clear up after another little mess like the one you left last time. If he displeases you, don't use a knife again, try poison, it's far less messy and takes a little longer to detect. Anyway, how are things proceeding over at the coast?" he asked. "Very well. The location is as near perfect as it can be, as you'll have seen from my report. It's a near-derelict Victorian house with stables in thick woodland and is accessed via a single-track lane from the main road. The beauty of it is there's a local feed power line quite close by and the roof of the stables is in pretty good order."

Her boss, Mario, was of Cuban heritage, his pro-American parents being kicked out of Cuba following Fidel Castro's 1950s revolution, but she always called him Uncle. "And how's the sale proceeding, because I think you said there was an issue?" he asked. "There was, because the absentee owner, who lives permanently in the south of France, suddenly decided not to sell, so I'm securing the place on a long-term lease which is far better for us. His lawyers are in Sheffield, so all the legal stuff has been done via the net and I received the tenancy agreement in the post this morning," she explained. "So how long before the setup team could move in?" he asked. "Probably in about three weeks and after that I'll lift our boys from wherever they are and settle them in, with a nice bonus to keep them sweet."

Tanya Talbot's life story, as told to Royston, was largely true up to the point where she'd been left her fortune, but that was not true. Her rags to riches fiction only served as the cover story under which, she was able to flit around the country keeping a watchful eye on the syndicate's various cannabis growing and drug dealing operations and seeking out potential new sites, while 'having some fun' with the odd lonely and vulnerable man she came across along the way, if the fancy took her.

It was she who'd first come across the old mill house in Little Oreford two years earlier and had rented it from its long absentee owners without involving estate agents, who might ask awkward questions and would always keep property details on their books.

Operations there had run so smoothly that she'd returned to the area, prior to the fire, and based herself in Draymarket, while looking for potential properties closer to the coast. It was while on her way back from checking out their latest site that she'd come across Royston's accident.

Chapter 16

To say that Royston had been quietly looking forward to his evening with Alicia would be an understatement and walking up the short drive to her front door in Cherry Grove, he felt like a dewy-eyed teenager on his first date. Alicia had also been looking forward to entertaining Royston and had quietly made up her mind that if she still liked him by the end of the evening, then she might end up in bed with him. It had been quite a while since she'd enjoyed the intimate company of a man, apart from her old college friend, Peter, whom she still met up with occasionally and was due to see the following weekend. Her front door opened as he approached, because she'd been hovering by the small window beside it and had already spotted him coming, bearing flowers and a bottle of bubbly, still quite chilled from its short journey from the village's open all hour's store.

"I wasn't sure whether to bring wine or bubbly, but, seeing it's such a lovely warm evening, I plumped for Champagne." Alicia said he'd a made perfect choice.

"I've already set flutes out on the patio table because I too had planned on bubbly, but we can save mine for another time," she said taking his jacket and leading him through the small neat kitchen and out into the garden. 'So, if all went well there was going to be 'another time' and that thought excited him. Sitting him down, she disappeared, quickly returning with a bowl of olives and some finely sliced wholemeal bread to accompany a shallow dish of balsamic and olive oil. "This is where I'll probably disgrace myself by dripping oil down my shirt," he said smiling at her. "I could always tie a linen napkin around your neck."

They'd gently probed one another's background during their first evening together in The Lion, so now he started telling her all about his pending acquisition of Gibbs and Sons. "How exciting and is this going to be a one-off expansion or might you later try and takeover other rival agencies operating on the borders of your newly expanded territory?" she asked. "To be honest I haven't even given that a thought, but I'm getting quite a buzz out of all of this so, who knows?" he answered. "So what have you been up to today?" she asked.

A coolness suddenly stole over the small garden as the sun slid behind a neighbouring property, so they went inside where Royston was seated at the table in her small dining room, while Alicia disappeared into the kitchen to put the finishing touches to their supper. "I hope you don't mind, it's only poached salmon with new potatoes and a mixed salad," she called. "To have a meal cooked for me is a real treat and I can never say no to salmon in all its forms."

When supper was over, they retired to the living room, where Royston took the armchair and Alicia settled on the sagging sofa and they continued their putting the world to rights conversation, which had begun at the dining table. It seemed they shared similar views on most things and were reaching the stage of feeling relaxed and comfortable in each other's company, when Alicia got up to make the coffee in the kitchen and decided she would not be taking Royston to bed, even if he was willing.

She knew that when she and Peter met up the following Saturday in their usual country house hotel, midway between their homes, they'd pretty soon end up in bed together and that, she now concluded, would not be fair on Royston had she slept with him the previous week. Alternatively, if she did climb into bed with him, she could always cry off on Peter claiming a migraine and, as she was a sufferer, she knew this occasionally used excuse would be accepted. But she was looking forward to meeting up with him again.

"I was wondering if you might like to come out with me for a test drive in my newly repaired classic car on Sunday of next week," he invited once she had poured the coffee. "Oh, what was the matter with it?" she answered, so deflecting the invitation.

He told her the whole story, well not quite the whole story because he made no mention of Tanya Talbot, other than that a woman motorist had raised the alarm. "Sadly, I'm not around next weekend as I'm meeting up with Peter, an old college friend, who I see a couple of times a year, but I'm free the following weekend and would love to come out for a drive. Maybe I could make a picnic and we could go to the coast for the day." Alicia didn't have to mention Peter, but he was a more or less permanent fixture in her so far quite itinerant life so, if she was going to have a relationship with Royston, then he'd have to know about Peter. Hopefully her offer of the picnic would have compensated for her revealing there was another man in her life.

Royston said he'd love for them to spend that Sunday together, as Saturday was a working day, and that he was looking forward to it already. They arranged that he'd pick her up around 10am, but would call earlier to finalise arrangements. He left shortly afterwards, having given her a hug and a kiss on the cheek on her doorstep.

He thought a lot about their evening together as he drove slowly home and was excited about what would be their third date, but then he began wondering about this Peter and whether this relationship was more than just a long-standing friendship. If she was seeing Peter next weekend then there was really no reason why he shouldn't see Tanya, now was there?

Chapter 17

"Mum, can we go out to play in the back garden?" asked Lottie after breakfast that Sunday morning. "Yes, but put your boots on because the grass is still wet." Laura was listening to The Archers; she'd been an addict since childhood, when glancing out of the kitchen window, she spotted Luke and Lottie standing by the gap in the hedge, which Ben had still not blocked, appearing to be talking to someone.

Could it be that woman who'd been hanging around the place?' In an instant she was on full alert and with all the raw protective instincts of a lioness for her cubs, she was dashing out of the house, down the steps and racing towards them. "Luke, Lottie come here," she shouted. The children turned towards her, surprise writ large on their young faces. "Who were you talking to?" she demanded. "No one, Mum," said Luke, a startled look in his eyes. "We were watching a squirrel on that branch over there." Relief welled up inside, but Laura's heart was still pounding. "Oh, how silly of me, children, I thought it was that lady, who looks a bit like me."

Lottie suddenly remembered their last game of hide and seek. "You mean the one who started talking to me the other day when we were playing in the garden?" said Lottie, having completely forgotten she hadn't told her mum about that! Again, Laura felt a fear rising inside her. "When was this and why didn't you tell me about it at the time?" There was a sharpness in her voice and Lottie started crying. Laura was instantly sorry and swept her daughter into her arms, fighting back her own tears as she did so. "It's all right, Mum," said Luke suddenly stretching out a protective arm. "Oh, children, I'm sorry for frightening you like that, but you know you mustn't talk to strangers and must always come and tell me or daddy if anyone comes into the garden and starts talking to you. Come on let's all go inside and I'll find a special treat."

Ben had driven down to Hampton Green for the Sunday papers and was ordered to go out and plug the gap in the hedge as soon as he returned. "It's a job that's needed doing for weeks and I really would like you to get on with it today," she said.

It wasn't until the children had gone up to bed that Laura told Ben about that morning's incident with the squirrel and just how much it had frightened her and how Lottie had then admitted she'd spoken earlier to the lady who looked like her.

162

"I don't like mysteries, especially ones that have got me on edge and could possibly be a real threat to our children. It's the only thing that's casting a shadow over our new life, here," she admitted. "OK" said Ben. "Robin was probably right when he assumed that she might live in Yardley, because it's only a short walk away down across the fields, so on my next day off, I'll go around the village with your picture asking everyone if they recognise the image." She smiled at the thought of him wandering around and stopping people. "What will you do if someone does, Ben?" she asked. "If that happens and I find out where she's living, we'll both go around and confront her and tell her never to come near us or our home again," he promised. "Oh, Ben, you make it sound so simple," she sighed. "Well, maybe it will be. Come on, I'm feeling like an early night. Let's go to bed." Laura suddenly picked up one of their sofa cushions and threw it at him. "I know you and your early nights. They usually become quite late ones!"

Laura had not long been at her desk in Randall's that Monday morning when Royston came in and she got up to make his coffee. Hannah was at the Draymarket branch, while Heather was now staffing the temporary advance sales office, which had just gone up on the

163

Greenfield Park building site at the edge of town. Laura had earlier dropped the kids off at school and because it was their first morning back after the summer holidays, Lottie was a little apprehensive at having 'gone up' into Miss Wiltshire's class.

Royston stood in the window nursing his mug of coffee and peering out over the top of the house ads to see who was coming and going along the street, a habit he'd got into over the years. "Here's a bit of news that will interest you, Laura." She looked up from her desk expectantly. "Yes, I was up at Little Oreford on Friday measuring up the old coaching inn, for which we now have the sale instructions, and would you believe it, the original bar is still in situ because when it was converted into a house, the former owners couldn't bring themselves to smash it up so they made it a feature of a huge living room."

Now Laura really was interested! "It's been used as a holiday home for years, but now the Hubbard's, who live in Ipswich, have decided to sell because they're not managing to get over here much these days."

Laura was about to say she might have a buyer, but thought better of it, deciding instead to call Robin just as soon as Royston was out of the office. But what on earth would Margo say because he'd been teasing her about making a bid for the inn for weeks.

Royston was in an optimistic mood because the new development sales office had only been open a week and already half a dozen people had been in and expressed a serious interest in buying off-plan; secondly, the Gibbs and Sons merger was proceeding a lot more smoothly than expected and thirdly, he'd fixed another date with Tanya, having called and chatted to her for over an hour the previous evening.

He'd continued to rationalise that if Alicia was going to spend a weekend with her 'friend' Peter, then there was no earthly reason why he shouldn't see Tanya, who'd invited him around to her place on the coming Friday evening.

Alek and Danek had not ventured far from Broadway Villas over the weekend, keeping themselves to themselves and talking quietly over all that had happened to them in the past couple of weeks. They'd escaped from the fire with only the clothes they were wearing and neither had their mobile phones with them, so it had been impossible to contact their employers and get picked up. But they had their well-rehearsed cover story in case of a raid or some other emergency, so after

165

a miserable night spent in an empty barn, they'd given themselves up. All had gone surprisingly well and latterly they'd also been caught off-guard by the unexpected kindnesses being shown to them by the people of Draymarket. They both knew they'd been totally complicit in the old mill cannabis growing operation and that it was not their first location, but they also reflected how they'd been slowly seduced into the racket with large cash rewards, a serious amount of which they had been able to send home.

It had all begun innocently enough after the two friends had come legally to work in the UK and had answered a social media site ad for agricultural migrant workers. But after a couple of weeks tending plants in an old barn in a remote situation, they began realising all was not quite as it seemed and that was when they should have walked away. But the situation had already become complicated, because they'd both ended up in bed together with their employer, a blonde, slim and highly attractive young woman, who was partnered by an older man, who she simply referred to as her uncle.

It was suggested after a while that if they joined her and uncle and their associates in this little cannabis growing venture, then they would make a considerable amount of money. And if the 'farm' they were operating should ever be raided, which was most unlikely given the high level of security imposed, then they could simply claim to have been enticed in as slave labour and would probably get away with it, they were assured.

The two were by no means stupid and realised with a stark clarity that if they tried to withdraw, they'd more than likely be prevented from doing so. They'd already been graphically treated to a little demonstration that their highly-charged young boss could probably be ruthless, on the night she'd got them high on booze and into bed with her and had then produced a knife to 'spice up' their little sex games, as she'd put it.

But with all that had happened to them over recent days, neither were sure they wanted to be picked up and transferred to another project. So, when Jackie Benson arrived and suggested they might like to go fruit picking on a nearby farm, receive a wage and be among fellow immigrant workers, with accommodation included, they willingly agreed.

This would give them a breathing space while they applied to their consulate for replacement passports, 'lost' in the fire, after which they would disappear back to Poland. The chances were that their employers, who'd insisted on keeping their original passports as security, would by now have found out about the damage to the mill and would most likely have backed off, leaving them in the clear.

It was the following Friday morning that Ben set out carrying a picture of Laura he'd printed out from his laptop.

He strolled down through the fields to Yardley Upton. There was a coolness in the air, the hay crop had been safely gathered in and autumn would be on the way. His hands still bore the slight stains of blackberry juice from their family foraging along the hedge rows just behind the house the previous evening.

An old wooden footbridge over a weed filled drainage ditch at the bottom of the hill led into a field, normally occupied by grazing Friesian cows, but now it was empty and dotted about him were the tell-tale white smudges of field mushrooms which had sprung up overnight.

What a bounty and only him there to pick them! Feeling the little surge of excitement that had always accompanied the spotting of mushrooms ever since he was a kid growing up in the country, he reached for the knapsack he was carrying, because Laura had asked him to pick up a pint of milk from the village store.

168

Stooping and gently squeezing the soft base of the stalk between two fingers, he eased the first of a whole crop of mushrooms out of the earth and gently placed it in his sack as the fungi delivered up just a hint of its distinctive fragrance. Twenty minutes later with a bag full of his bounty, he emerged into the village street and straight away came across the local postman, probably the best person to ask other than the lady who kept the village store. "No. Can't say I've seen her around here, but why are you asking?" There was a note of suspicion in his voice. "It's a bit of a mystery really in that several people, who know my wife, have told her they've seen this woman around here, who looks remarkably like her, so we thought we'd see if we could find her, if only to satisfy our curiosity."

When Ben entered the village shop, its door and windows plastered with small adverts and notices, he was relieved to see it was empty. It would be one thing discreetly showing Laura's picture over the counter, but quite another, passing it around a gaggle of gossiping customers and causing a bit of a scene.

"Oh, yes, I know who that is," came the instant response, catching Ben totally off his guard. "That's Corinne. She's the lass who helps out over at Edwards farm where they grow all the fruit and vegetables for the supermarkets and she's often in here picking up supplies.

They could always get all they need delivered in from Draymarket, but Jimmy Edwards, who's our parish council chairman, is a great believer in supporting the local community and, to tell you the truth, I'm not sure I'd be able to keep going without him and his seasonal workers, who are always popping in. It's also the reason why I keep open all hours because I live above the shop and I'd hate to think of those boys and girls walking for around two miles to find me closed."

Ben emerged in a quandary. He'd never expected to find the mystery woman and was only really doing this to satisfy Laura, so now what was he going to do? To start with, he wasn't going to walk two miles and back to the farm, so he might as well go home and besides, his mushrooms needed putting in the fridge. He was almost back before remembering he'd forgotten to buy the milk. Making himself a black coffee, and carrying his mug out onto the rear patio, he sat on the step and was just wondering what to do next when Robin emerged from around the side of the house. "Just the man! Here sit down and I'll get you a coffee. I think there's probably enough milk left in the bottle."

Twenty minutes later, they'd made a plan. Rather than waiting until after work, they'd drive down to the farm now and see, whether they could get a brief word with this Corinne, depending on the circumstances.

The wide paved farm track branching off the country road, roughly west of Yardley Upton, led along a small valley, slowly opening up into a large shallow bowl in the hills, now under full and intensive cultivation. Pulling into a substantial layby just ahead, Ben stopped the car. "I had no idea all this was here," he said, leaning his forearms on the wheel. "Me neither and, just to think, it can't be more than three miles from us as the crow flies," agreed Robin.

To their left were literally hundreds of rows of fruit bushes on the side of the hill, below which were line upon line of polytunnels.

Ahead appeared to be the main farm complex and rising gently beyond and to the right was a succession of giant fields now showing a vast shimmer of early winter greens.

Should they turn around there and come back that evening? asked Ben. "No, come on. Let's go for it, but I suggest we first make inquiries at the farm office because a setup this size is bound to have one, and we can't really go wandering around without permission," said Robin.

Arriving at the farm gate, they quickly spotted a worker, who directed them along a side road with rows of portacabins, clearly the accommodation, and then, right out of the blue, synchronicity lent a helping hand. On rounding a gentle bend, there on the right-hand side of the road was Laura's double.

She was standing with two vaguely familiar looking young men and while recovering from the shock of seeing just how like Laura she was, they realised the two were the Polish workers they'd rescued from the old mill house.

Ben pulled up beside them and leaned out of the window. "Are you Corinne?" He was smiling as he asked the question, but then spotted a dawning recognition on the face of one of the young men, standing hesitantly beside her.

"That's right, I am Corinne, but I don't think I know you, do I?"

Her face was colouring with the first hint of embarrassment, although she didn't know why. Now

172

Alek was peering in through the windscreen at Ben and then across at Robin.

"You are the ones who rescued us from the fire," he declared. "We are, but we've come to hopefully have a word with Corinne here," Ben said looking up expectantly at her and still smiling. There was an awkward silence. "Look, I can't imagine why you should want to see me, but if you'll give me a couple of minutes while I finish what I'm doing, then we can talk."

She directed them to the staff car park just up ahead and, noticing a picnic table with benches close by, they settled down to wait.

The young woman reappeared shortly afterwards and casually took the seat opposite. 'She even walks like Laura,' Ben thought. "Now, how can I help you?" she said, smiling disarmingly in just the way that Laura did and again shaking Ben.

"So what do you make of this?" he said, slowly placing Laura's picture in front of her. "Oh my God, it's me, but no, it's not me!" she exclaimed. "No Corinne you're right. It's not you. It's my wife, Laura, who's on edge because our children have spotted you several times loitering around our home, Albany House up at Little Oreford."

173

Putting emphasis on the word 'home,' he looked straight into her eyes as he did so.

"Oh! I'm so embarrassed, I don't know what to say."

Ben suddenly felt sorry for her and his voice softened. "Perhaps you might start by telling me why you are so interested in Albany House?" But nothing could have prepared them for her answer!

"It's because I believe my mother was born there, so I wanted to look at the house and imagine her playing in the garden."

Robin felt his heart missing a beat. So could this be Charlie's daughter and Laura's twin, who'd suddenly turned up right of the blue and in an instant, he was back in the garden of their childhood playing a game of dares with her mum.

And, good heavens, why hadn't he noticed just how like Charlie, Laura was after all this time? Hadn't Margs said soon after they'd first met Laura that she reminded her of someone. And to think, they'd even remarked how much Laura looked like the Rev Will Potter's wife Anne in that old photograph.

Ben was also coming to the incredible conclusion that Corinne was Laura's twin. "So would you mind telling us your surname?" he asked quietly. "Yes, I'm Corinne

Potter and I believe from looking at the list of previous rectors in The Little Oreford parish church, that I must have been the last incumbent's granddaughter!" she told him.

Now a stunned silence filled the space between them and then shattered by a farm vehicle passing by "This is almost too incredible for words because from all you have said, you must surely be my wife, Laura's twin! She was adopted from the Bristol nursing home, where she was born, by a couple called Ellerbie, whose surname she was given, so she never knew her birth mother's name. But given your remarkable likeness to her and the fact that you both look so much like your grandmother, Anne, I think there can be little doubt that Laura's real surname is also Potter and that she has a twin sister we never knew existed."

Before she could answer, the 'walkie talkie' she'd placed on the table sprang into life: "Corinne, to the office please!"

She picked it up. "Look I have to go now and I really do need some time to think about all of this," she said rising from the table, her face red with embarrassment.

"Wait a minute. Will you come up for tea around 4pm on Saturday and meet Laura and our children, who unless I am wildly mistaken, are your niece and nephew?"

Corinne hesitated for a moment and then accepted the invitation.

Chapter 18

As Laura drove Luke and Lottie to school the following
morning there was still only one thing on her mind. That
was that her grandfather was almost certainly the Rev
Will Potter and that her mother was Robin and Margo's
wayward family playmate, Charlie Potter, and that on
Saturday, she would be coming face-to-face with the
twin sister she never knew she had.

Once she'd recovered from the initial shock, she and
Ben had gone straight over to Robin and Margo's to
have another look at the old photograph album with the
picture of the Rev Will Potter's wife, Anne. It had only
taken one look through Robin's magnifying glass to
reaffirm that Anne with her short hair and elfin-like looks
was indeed her and Corinne's grandmother.

But what Laura was also finding difficult to come to
terms with was the fact that by pure coincidence, she
and Ben had actually come to live so close to Little
Oreford and that she had been so compulsively drawn to
Albany House.

She was not alone in being preoccupied that morning
because Royston was also looking forward, a little guiltily
and apprehensively, to his dinner date with Tanya in her

flat that evening. But both had a compelling reason to ditch their distractions shortly afterwards, when a smart suited lawyer walked in to Randall's with instructions to dispose of the old mill house in Little Oreford. His client, who lived in the Isle of Man, had asked him to seek the best price possible for the fire damaged property for which he now needed a valuation, prior to putting it on the market. Randall's would waive their valuation fee and charge a reduced commission if they were given sole agency status, Royston suggested. This cut no ice with the lawyer, who, having already looked around the property, was rather of the opinion that it should be advertised by one of the big national agencies because whether or not any money was saved on agency fees, was of little interest to him.

Laura, sitting quietly at her desk, surprised both herself and Royston by suddenly entering the conversation. "But just to remind you, Mr Randall, we already have a potential cash buyer very interested in acquiring the property, so there would be no need for it to even go on the market once a valuation had been agreed."

Now she had their full attention and the surprised look on Royston's face was palpable, but he knew better than to query her. "Of, course we have. How stupid of me to have forgotten, Laura." The lawyer indicated that a quick private sale was the best possible outcome and after instructing Royston to proceed with a valuation, he produced a heavy set of keys from his case, presented his card and left. "So, what do you know that I don't?" asked Royston the minute the door closed. Laura had previously felt it best not to reveal she knew Robin was interested in Little Oreford's former coaching inn and possibly the mill, out of loyalty to Margo, who was still not keen on the idea, but now she was being put on the spot. She took a deep breath. "As you know, the Lloyds purchased Albany House so that we could rent it from them and we've all become close friends so, naturally, I knew of their desire to buy the old coaching inn, for which they now have a viewing, and I also know that they might want to acquire the mill." Then why hadn't she mentioned this before? Royston wondered.

"It's not for me to divulge their plans to anyone because it's their business, so I should never have spoken out of turn just now." Royston saw instantly she'd been put in a spot between her loyalty to her friends and her desire to help him.

"OK, as far as I'm concerned, we've not had this conversation. All you have to do is to tell Mr Lloyd of this

179

morning's visitation and that the property is to be valued prior to going on the market and then it's entirely up to him what happens next."

After supper that evening while Ben was getting the kids to bed, Laura popped over to Robin's and Margo's and was immediately invited to join them for their customary pre-dinner drink because the only topic of conversation on their minds was the forthcoming Saturday tea with Corinne.

"The last we heard of your mum was before she'd gone off to Bristol University, so perhaps your dad had been there too?" suggested Robin. "Of course, we came back to the village many times to see our mum and dad, but when we asked if they'd heard anything of Charlie, the answer was always no," Margo explained. "Our parents were agnostics and never went anywhere near the church, so I suppose that was understandable," she said.

"I suppose Randall's must be pretty busy at the moment what with the merger and the new Draymarket housing estate," said Robin, suddenly changing the subject. "Oh yes and you'll never guess what happened today," replied Laura. now given the perfect opportunity of raising the matter she had come to discuss, without feeling disloyal to Margo.

Robin's instant reaction on hearing the old mill house might now be within his grasp was one of undisguised jubilation, but Margo was not nearly so sure. She'd gone along with him over Laura's surprise news that the village's former coaching inn was coming up for sale, because they could rent that out for the time being, but acquiring a seriously damaged former mill that was going to cost tens of thousands to repair was a completely different matter.

Luckily for Margo, the oven timer buzzer told them their casserole was ready and abruptly ended the conversation. While Laura was strolling back across the green, Royston was on his way into Draymarket and looking forward to his evening with Tanya, while images of Alicia floating disconcertingly around in the back of his mind. "I really shouldn't be doing this," he said aloud. A faint aroma of incense greeted him as he climbed the stairs to her apartment and she answered the door dressed in a colourful blue sari. "Come in darling. I'm preparing one of my favourite Indian Tandoori dishes and I thought I'd get into the mood.

"I couldn't resist buying several saris in one of those amazingly colourful markets in India that completely assault all your senses. Have you been there?" she asked, opening her eye level fridge and pulling out two cans of beer. "I'm afraid not. I've been pretty unadventurous when it comes to holidays."

Tanya said they'd have to change that.

Again, a fleeting vision of Alicia floated into his mind as he took the beer and pulled its metal tab. She'd closed the heavy drape curtains and dimmed the lights just a little and the sweet aroma, he noticed, was drifting in a thin taper of smoke from a joss stick on the coffee table. "When I prepare one of my favourite Indian dishes, I like to create an atmosphere," she said, leading him into the kitchen where the ambience was immediately banished by an unforgiving white strip light, about which she could do little.

The extensively modernised kitchen contained one of those fashionable central food preparation stations, now displaying a large chopping board with an array of peppers, chilly's and other necessary vegetables beside which several sharp knives gleamed in the fluorescent light.

Tanya ordered him to sit on one of the high level stools while she quickly donned a floral apron, rather clashing with the sari, he thought, as he removed his jacket.

"That's right, darling, do make yourself comfortable. You can help chop up the ingredients, or just watch, it's up to you." Royston elected to watch.

"So, what have you been up to this week?" she asked. He told her all about the progress of his merger with Gibbs and Sons and how successful the new estate sales office had been in its first week and how he'd just been asked to value an old mill house up at Little Oreford where there had been a fire.

"You might have heard about that. It's been all over the news recently, because when the firefighters and the police arrived, they discovered the building had been used for growing cannabis and the two men who'd been growing it ran off, but were later arrested."

Tanya, who was busy emptying her now finely chopped ingredients into a large pan, said it all sounded very exciting. "Do you think I could come along with you when you do your valuation? I'd love to see inside the place, which has been a crime scene!" Her sudden request took him by surprise, but thinking about it, there was really no reason why she shouldn't accompany him.

"Now, just how hot do you like your curries?" she asked.
After the meal, she suggested they watch one of her
favourite movies, which to his embarrassment, turned
out to be highly erotic and on the theme of bondage.
"Perhaps we should try a little play acting of our own,"
she said after it had reached its climax and she was
leading him by the hand, and not altogether unwillingly,
towards her bedroom.

Chapter 19

Corinne Potter, who like Laura, had been thinking of little else other than the incredible fact that she was about to be reunited with the twin sister she never knew she had, finished work at lunchtime on the Saturday. She had the luxury of a bath in her apartment and took a long soak to recover from a hot morning out on the farm.

Oh, how far she'd come since being given up for adoption, but infact, spending seven years in a children's home before going on to live with a succession of well meaning foster parents in and around Bristol and latterly in the nearby Victorian town of Clevedon.

The only constant in her life had been her birth mother's quite battered red leather shoulder bag, inside of which was a letter for her to open once she was old enough to read. The bag could have gone astray on any number of occasions, but somehow and quite miraculously, it had remained with her. Other children had their favourite cuddly toys, but Corinne had her bag and it seldom, if ever, left her side.

The letter, together with a small black and white photograph, had been tucked deep inside an inner pocket and had somehow avoided detection, until one

185

day when Corinne, now in her early teens and feeling particularly unhappy, had suddenly taken it out of her cupboard as a comforter.

'My dearest, dearest little Corinne I have tried so hard to keep you, but, in the end, I have failed, but please, please try and remember that I will always love you,' it read.

The picture showed three children in the garden of a large house and on the back were the words 'Albany House, Little Oreford.'

She had been all on her own for the whole of her life, but now it seemed she had a twin sister a brother-in-law, who seemed really nice and a young niece and nephew. Corinne dressed and decided that as it was such a lovely afternoon, she would stroll up though the fields to Little Oreford, carrying her treasured shoulder bag in the large backpack she used when walking into Yardley to pick up her personal supplies from the village shop. The bag itself was encased in its own protective heavy duty plastic wallet and had remained that way for some years. She'd worked in London in the heady high-powered world of advertising for most of her twenties and early thirties, sharing apartments with female colleagues and having several quite long-term relationships. But they'd always come to a parting of the ways because in every case, living together had not worked for her. She'd read loads of books on relationships, trying to rationalise her feelings, before eventually coming to the conclusion that because she'd had such an unsettled upbringing, she'd developed a protective shell, so much so that she would allow men so far into her life but no further.

Then she really thought she'd turned a corner with Tony, an up-and-coming senior partner in her own organisation, but again it had all gone horribly wrong leaving her feeling she had no alternative other than to resign.

The experience left her depressed and traumatised and that was when she decided on a complete change of life style.

She would now go and do what she had been putting off doing for many years and that was to find Little Oreford and finally go in search of her roots. 'So just why had she put it off for so long?' she asked herself. The reason, she supposed, was that given the transient nature of her childhood, she had always preferred looking forward rather than back.

It had been surprisingly easy to find a job as an assistant manager on a large fruit and vegetable farm just down the road from Little Oreford. Corinne bonded with farm owner, Jimmy Edwards, almost immediately. He found her willingness to take on any task and to learn all she could about his large enterprise a breath of fresh air after his last assistant manager. On her first day off, she'd walked up through the fields to Little Oreford and had gone straight to the parish church, where she quickly discovered that her grandfather must have been the last full-time rector.

Now on that fateful Saturday afternoon, she had reached the top of the fields and, walking along the footpath behind Albany House, discovered that the convenient gap in the hedge, which had allowed her to look in on the property, had been blocked and that made her feel guilty. No matter, because in just a few minutes she'd be walking along its wide gravelled drive and knocking on the front door and would have another opportunity to apologise for spying on the family.

Long before the appointed hour, Laura was hovering in the doorway. She wanted to be alone when she met Corinne and that had been easily arranged because Ben had taken the kids off to a birthday party in Hampton Green.

Robin and Margo had agreed not to come over until 4.30pm.

The distinctive chimes of the church clock were half way through striking the hour when Laura spotted her twin coming into sight around the corner from the footpath and stepped out of the porch to meet her. Corinne had also seen Laura and could feel her heart beginning to beat as she walked slowly up the drive towards her. Both women, now only a few steps apart, stopped and stared at their mirror images. Time stood still. Then as one, they rushed forward and in floods of tears, embraced and hugged. It was as if all their shared emotions and deep feelings of abandonment had suddenly found their longed-for release and they both somehow felt whole again.

"There's so much to talk about and to share that I just don't know where to begin," said Laura, after they'd both recovered, and she was leading the way through the house and out onto the patio, where she'd laid the table for tea and they both sat down. Corinne said she knew just where to begin and that was by apologising for spying and worrying them all rather than just coming and knocking on the door.

"But just imagine if you had and we'd come face to face. What a shock that would have been," countered Laura. "At least the way it worked out, we've both had time to come to terms with the fact that we had a twin," she added. "I know, but I should have come anyway, instead of skulking about in the bushes, but the truth is something just held me back and I can't really explain it," she admitted. "No need to now," said Laura, looking past Corinne to see Ben emerging from the kitchen door. Corinne turned, hearing a movement behind her. "So, you two have met at last, have you?" he said slipping into the seat next to Laura. It seemed such an inane and obvious thing to say, but he didn't really know what else he could have said in the circumstances. "Indeed, we have," replied Laura, looking up to see Robin and Margo coming around the side of the house rather than just walking in through the front door as they would normally have done.

Everyone stood up as they approached carrying their old family album and Robin introduced Margo to Corinne. Margo just stared at Laura and Corinne standing side by side for the first time.

"It really is quite remarkable just how alike you are and to be perfectly honest, Laura, if you were both dressed identically, I'm honestly not sure that I could tell you apart," she declared. "So where should we begin?" Ben asked after they'd all sat down and Margo had placed the family album on the table in front of her.

"I think I should begin by telling you all how I found my way to Little Oreford," said Corinne. It didn't take long and when she'd finished, she leant down and carefully removed the sealed plastic wallet from her backpack. "And here is our mother's red leather shoulder bag, which has miraculously reunited us after so many years," she said, carefully opening it, drawing out the photograph and placing it on the table placed in front of them. "Oh, my goodness, Margo, it's us with Charlie and it's just like the one we have," said Robin, opening their album to reveal an almost identical picture.

Corinne just stared at it, the last single shred of doubt that this could all be a huge coincidence, dispelled forever. "Now there is something else for you to see Laura," she said, again opening the red shoulder bag and carefully drawing out their mother's letter, now protected in its own envelope and handing it over to her twin. 'My dearest, dearest little Corinne," Laura read aloud, already feeling her heart aching with emotion and the tears welling up all over again. "I have tried so hard to keep you but, in the end, I have failed, but please, please try and remember that I will always love you." Putting the letter down on the table, Laura began drying her eyes with the tissue Margo had handed her. "So, I guess our mother must have been unmarried, a terrible thing in those days, and gave me up at birth, but tried to keep you," she said quietly "Now we have found one another we must try and find out what happened to her, we must and I won't rest until we do," she resolved. "We really will Laura," Corinne agreed. "But now you must tell me how you and Ben found your way back to Little Oreford," she said. "That was pure coincidence because we came to live nearby. Then a very strange thing happened because when I came to have a viewing of Albany House, which was up for sale, I met Margo on the green. She invited me in for coffee and showed me her photograph album containing old photos of the village and inside was this picture," she said, asking Robin to find the page and show it to Corinne. "There's your grandfather, the Rev Will Potter, with your grandmother, Anne, and can you see how alike both you and Laura are to her," said Robin.

"We spotted the likeness between me and Anne Potter at the time, but simply put it down to a pure

192

coincidence," said Laura. "So, I suppose it's time to tell you what happened to me after I was adopted by Frank and Joyce Ellerbe," she said. "The problem is, I never really got to know them, because when I was four, my stepdad, who was a civil engineer, went off to work on a six month aid project in Nigeria and my step mum went out to join him for a holiday leaving me with her mum and dad. But they were both killed in a car accident, leaving me to be raised by my step grandparents in Solihull, near Birmingham," Laura explained.

"I passed my Eleven Plus, which was the big exam in those days, and went to the local grammar school and then on to university, where I met Ben at a Fresher's Fair and the rest as they say is history." Then Robin told Corinne how their mum, who'd always insisted on being called Charlie, rather than Charlotte, had always been their leader when he and Margo were growing up. "We'd be in the middle of playing one game, or building a den in the woods or something, when she'd suddenly get tired of it and we'd be straight on to the next thing," he said. "It was a pretty idyllic childhood because our parents allowed us to run wild from dawn to dusk roaming the surrounding countryside and Charlie always

193

managed to 'escape' from her more restrictive surroundings to be our leader.

But like all good things it came to a parting of the ways when we left to take up careers in London and Charlie, we think went off travelling before going to Bristol University, and sadly our paths never crossed again."

Corinne accepted their invitation to stay for supper and to meet Luke and Lottie after Ben had collected them from the party.

It was on the drive home from Draymarket that he broke the news to them that the lady, who'd spoken to Lottie in the garden that afternoon was actually their mum's long-lost sister and therefore their aunt.

"We don't need another aunt because we've got Margo now," Lottie retorted. She was confused because mummy was upset after she told her about the lady who looked like her and now daddy was saying she was actually mummy's sister.

Luke took the news without expressing any opinion because he was far more interested in the rubber band propelled glider that was in his party going home bag and which he would be putting together as soon as they got back.

While Ben was gone, Laura and Margo showed Corinne around the house, leaving Robin sitting on the patio, quietly turning things over in his ever-fertile mind. Corinne was obviously a bit of a wanderer, like her mum, but might she now want to stay closer to her roots and her new-found family? If she did, then might she not be the ideal person to run Broadway Villa as a B&B, after they'd acquired it because that was now in progress, and later be involved in its conversion back to an inn, he wondered.

She was clearly an organiser, hence her role down at the farm, so he'd raise the idea with her while he was driving her home, which he'd already volunteered to do. Luke and Lottie's party high had been deflated by Ben's news and they were both unusually quiet when they were introduced to Corinne, who interpreted their response as shyness.

It was as if they suddenly had two mums, one whom they knew intimately, and the other, about whom they knew nothing at all, and was going to be their aunt. Sensing their confusion, Corinne stepped forward and formally shook their hands saying that perhaps it might be better if she went home now, rather than staying for supper, because she'd had quite enough excitement for one day.

Chapter 20

Royston heard Tanya coming moments before she swept around the corner onto the Little Oreford green in her blue Mercedes sports coupe. 'My God, what a car,' he said to himself, standing, mesmerised as he watched her pull up behind his logoed Randall's estate and climbed out. She was wearing a clearly expensive dark three-quarter length coat and black leather boots and looked, quite frankly, stunning. He greeted her, clipboard in hand.

"What an amazing car. I had no idea you were an enthusiast. Why didn't you say something when I was telling you all about my poor old motor?" he asked, feeling slightly upstaged.

"I didn't like to, darling. It didn't seem appropriate seeing you'd just smashed up your pride and joy. Besides I'm not an enthusiast. I just like fast and flashy things."

Then another thought occurred to Royston. "Where on earth do you keep it?" he asked. "Oh, those nice people at Hendon Motors in town let me leave it in their large parking area."

What she omitted to tell him was that they also rented her one of their nondescript courtesy cars, now always on permanent standby should she need it for one of her little prospecting trips or some other business. The boss at Hendon couldn't understand why on earth she was happy to go on paying though the nose for one of his vehicles, when she could so easily have entered into a leasing agreement, which he'd suggested after a couple of weeks. Still, it was her money, so why should he care? It was while Royston was wrestling with the key to open the front gates to the mill house that Robin suddenly appeared.

He had a shrewd idea that Royston would be out on the Monday morning to do the valuation and he'd been keeping an eye open for them. 'There must be money in estate agency,' he thought, taking in the coupe, which he assumed belonged to Royston, rather than his attractive assistant, now holding the clipboard while he was finally opening the gate. Royston recognised Robin immediately as the purchaser of Albany House. "Don't say you're also interested in the mill as well as Broadway Villa," he asked, shaking hands with him and introducing Tanya as 'another interested party.' Just why he'd said that rather than that she was a friend, he wasn't sure, but it certainly amused her, considering she was a far more 'interested' party than he was ever likely to know.

Wandering slowly from room to room and ducking under ribbons of tape, which the police had forgotten to remove, the sheer scale of the cannabis growing operation became self-evident even though all the hundreds of pots of plants had been removed and destroyed. The air had an acrid bitterness, the legacy of the fire which had left blackened ceilings and large scale scorch marks on all the walls and floors. "It's going to cost a packet to put this place back together again," said Robin, after they'd retreated down the main double staircase, which had luckily escaped any substantial damage.

But his spirits soared when, after walking through a large and lofty kitchen and anteroom, they entered the attached three-storey mill building over the stream to find all its ancient machinery largely intact. It was as if the doors to the mill had been closed in the early years of the 19th century and all inside forgotten, he thought. "What an amazing conservation project this would make," said Royston, gazing up at the clearly rotten oak planking. Tanya, who'd come in behind them, said nothing. She'd been in here with one of her people once before, but they'd only stayed long enough to realise that the lofty space would be no good for their purposes.

Once back outside, Robin and Tanya, again holding Royston's clipboard, now containing several pages of notes, hovered by his car while he struggled to turn the key in the rusting and unforgiving lock. "Would you like to come back for coffee?" Robin asked. Royston, his sights now firmly set on the prospect of a second surprise sale, said that would be good, but Tanya declined, claiming a prior engagement and telling Royston she'd be back in touch shortly, fixing 'her little rabbit' with a knowing look. Margo was out, but returned just as Robin and Royston had settled themselves at the kitchen table for an exploratory chat and realised instantly what was going on. "Come and join us, Margs, Mr Randall's here and hopefully he's going to tell us how much it's going to cost us to buy the old mill house." Margo disappeared to make the coffee before joining them, feeling just a little excited at the prospect of yet another new venture, despite her earlier misgivings. After all, once the property was acquired, they wouldn't actually have to do anything with it until Broadway Villa was paying its way, either as a B&B or a reopened inn. Just where did that couple get their money, Royston wondered on his drive to the Hampton Green office.

Still, provided the vendor accepted his valuation, that would be a tidy sum to go towards the Gibbs purchase. His mobile announced two incoming texts which he ignored until he was in the car park. The first was from Tanya inviting him up for 'a little more fun' the following evening because, as she reminded him, it was his turn to be tied to her bed! The second was from Alicia saying how much she was looking forward to their drive and picnic at the weekend and it ended with a kiss! So now what was he to do? He'd be kidding himself if he denied he was beginning to enjoy Tanya's exciting and totally unpredictable company and that she'd started breaking down his natural reserve. But to have another session with her and then to go on and take Alicia out for their drive and picnic was still a little too much for him to contemplate. The answer, he decided, was simple. He'd stall Tania until after the weekend, pleading pressure of work due to the forthcoming merger. 'After all you wouldn't want me tired out before we'd even started!' his reply text ended. "I thought we'd drive to the coast and have a walk and then our picnic, if the weather's reasonable that is," suggested Royston on the phone to Alicia that evening. It had been established on their first date that they both enjoyed walking and that was another little plus as far as Alicia was concerned.

The weather was kind to them when they set off, so they decided to take a leisurely drive through the lanes to Lynmouth. Royston knew the area well, but it was all refreshingly new to Alicia. "I thought we'd park in Lynmouth, have a coffee and then follow the lovely riverside path up to Waters Meet, where two rivers converge," he suggested.

"Sounds fine by me, but perhaps we could pop into a newsagent's so that I could pick up the local ordnance survey map, because I do like to see where I'm going and it could come in handy for future occasions!" The day flew by. They chatted and laughed, found a secluded spot for their picnic high above the river, lay on their backs and watched a pair of buzzards circling high overhead and began making their way back in the late afternoon. Royston had not enjoyed himself so much in a long time and the thought of spending another steamy night with Tanya had altogether lost its appeal. Should he take hold of Alicia's hand he wondered as they strolled along side by side greeting the occasional walker coming towards them? Was it too soon in their relationship and would he be courting rejection? 'Come on Royston, man up!' Heeding his father's words, he reached out and took her hand, which she held for a moment before giving it a gentle squeeze and letting it go.

It was as if a small cloud had suddenly drifted across a perfect afternoon sky, casting an embarrassing shadow over the promising horizon of his expectations. They chatted on, as if this small advance had never happened and, after stopping for a pub meal, pulled in to Cherry Grove in the late evening.

"Are you coming in?" she said turning towards him and giving him her soft slightly lopsided smile. He hesitated. "No, I think I'd better get back because I've got an early start tomorrow," he heard himself say, leaning over and planting a small kiss on her soft lips as he did so.

For some perverse reason, something in the egotistical side of his nature had needed to pay her back for her small rejection. "Shall we do this again, maybe next Sunday?" she asked as she turned to go. "Yes, that would be lovely," he replied, telling her he'd give her a call later in the week.

During their evening together, Alicia had regretted letting Royston's hand go. It had been a spur of the moment decision and she couldn't really account for it. Nothing was said, but she'd sensed his embarrassment in the tone of his voice immediately afterwards. Perhaps she'd done so because after their two nights together, Peter had told her he was tiring of their occasional long-distance relationship, which had suited him perfectly well up until then, and was considering quitting his post and finding another lecturing job in Bristol, which would mean they could see each other as often as they liked.

If Peter had suggested his change of plan a few weeks earlier, during one of their occasional evening phone calls, she would probably have welcomed it, but now she was not quite so sure and had decided to invite Royston in after all.

His polite rejection had taken her a little by surprise, but she could understand it and was disappointed by it.

'Why on earth didn't I go in?' Royston chided himself on his way home.

Just think, even now, they might be having a nightcap and she might be inviting him to spend the night with her. Still, they had a date for the following Sunday and hadn't she said when buying the map that it would be useful for future occasions, he consoled himself, but one thing he'd really now made up his mind about and that was to stop seeing Tanya.

Chapter 21

Robin decided he would sound Corinne out about her future after he had driven her back to the farm. "Can I share a confidence with you?" he asked, pulling into the car park they'd used before, and laying out all his plans for reopening the coaching inn and asking whether she might be prepared to become its manager. "I am enjoying working here for Jimmy, but what you have suggested all sounds absolutely amazing and, of course, you can count me in if it all goes ahead," she promised. Meanwhile Royston, now following up on his resolve to finish with Tanya, called her a couple of times with no response. The small coward in him was tempted to leave a message ending their relationship, but in the end, he did nothing. Then he received a text saying she was sorry she'd not got back to him, only something had come up which might take her out of town for a while. He didn't reply because hopefully this might be the end of their relationship without him having to go through the uncomfortable process of breaking it off.

The 'thing,' that had come' up, was her need to spend a lot more time on the final preparation and provisioning of her organisation's new site now that she'd signed the lease and her three man setup team were on their way down to do all the necessary work. Royston and Alicia took another trip to the coast the following Sunday. She'd been studying her new map and suggested they park in a small hamlet where the River Lyn, appeared from the contours, to open out into a wider area between hills. This, she understood, led to the Doone Valley, made famous by Lorna Doone, the romantic novel set on Exmoor.

Finding a convenient parking spot, not far from the river, they set out to explore, but had not been walking for more than an hour when the heavens threatened to open and luckily, they came upon a riverside pub. They'd only intended stopping for a sheltering pint, but as the rain had started and continued sending small rivulets down the curtained window beside them, they abandoned their sandwiches in favour of a bowl of soup.

"What's it like being back at school after the long break?" he asked. "A couple of days and you've forgotten you've even had a holiday." It was her stock answer to the polite question she'd been asked so many times before. "But there was one snippet that will interest you because it appears Laura Jameson has a twin sister, who suddenly turned up out of the blue! Her son, Luke, told the class all about it in our Show and Tell Time." Royston reminded her that Laura was a member of his village estate agency team, so he'd already heard the news. They stayed chatting in the pub until late in the afternoon before making their way back to his car and driving down into Lynmouth for supper. They spent much of the drive home in a companionable silence with Royston hoping she'd be inviting him in because if she did, he'd not be refusing this time.

"You will come in won't you?" she asked, turning towards him and kissing him on the lips after they'd pulled up in Cherry Grove.

She made them both a drinking chocolate, because it was more comforting and coffee tended to keep her awake, and then he was following her up the stairs, where they stood beside her full-length mirror, slowly undressing one another, interspersed with lingering kisses. "So, what shall we do next?" she asked when at last his boxer shorts had dropped to the floor. The directness of her question took Royston by surprise. "No one's ever asked me that before," he blustered, whereupon she sank to her knees in front of him. "So, would this be a good place to start?" she asked in her soft voice.

207

The set-up of the new cannabis production site had all gone according to plan with the gang's electrician managing to tap into the electricity supply from the power pole, close to the property, in order to supply all the necessary lights and lamps. Their carpenter had constructed the growing tables in all five large Victorian bedrooms and the spacious loft and had transformed the old drawing room into sleeping accommodation with the adjoining sitting room and kitchen becoming the mess area.

"The plants are all being delivered next week, Uncle, so I guess it's time to bring in our two gardeners," said Tanya on a call to her boss. "They're helping out on a big farm complex quite close to Draymarket, according to the local paper." How did she plan to extricate them without drawing attention to herself? he asked.

"I've thought about that and I think the answer is to write them a letter instructing them to meet me outside the village pub in Yardley Upton, which is only a couple of miles from the farm, say around 7pm next Monday."

Her boss said that sounded like a plan and, not being one for small talk, rang off. They'd operated together for five years and never once had he asked her how she was.

Tanya's letter came as a shock for the two, who, as she'd earlier feared, were beginning to hope their criminal life was behind them. She'd enticed them with a £5,000 bonus each and the promise they could always get out if they wanted to, once replacement gardeners had been found. They had no doubt the bonuses would be paid because they'd always been well remunerated to keep them sweet.

It had been the organisation's view that slave labourers were a risk because they could always run away and keeping a constant watch on them was a hassle, but if they were paid, they were far more likely to be both willing and compliant and an asset rather than a risk. But Alek and Danek seriously doubted that once they'd been drawn back into the ring, they'd ever be allowed to leave. Besides that, they'd already played their slave labour card and had been believed, but that was never going to happen again if the place were ever raided. No, they'd applied for new passports to replace the ones, which they claimed had been destroyed in the mill fire, they were earning reasonable money and as soon as they'd saved enough for their airfare, they'd be going home. Both had acquired quite a considerable sum from the cash they'd sent home and were now planning to go into business together, although they'd yet to decide what it would be.

It was agreed that Danek would walk into the village to meet Tanya and tell her they were not coming back and to swear there was no way they'd ever betray the ring because they'd probably end up in jail if they did. "We'll be out of the UK in a couple of months at the latest and, trust me, we're never coming back," he told her through her open car window before turning on his heels and walking slowly away.

"We have a problem, Uncle, and it's going to hold up production," she called and told him as she watched Danek disappear into the distance.

Chapter 22

Jimmy Edwards was, by necessity, an early riser. He'd spent the past couple of hours on paperwork in his office and had just finished breakfast up at 'the big house,' as his workers called it, when his farm manager gave a cursory knock on the back kitchen door and burst in with the shock news that his two latest recruits had been found dead in their cabin. Hurrying to the scene, he found a small crowd hovering around the open door as if the macabre happening inside had some perverse attraction. Jimmy ignored them and it only took one step into the room to see both blood-stained bodies sprawled side by side on their single beds. The shock of it sent him backwards out of the cabin where he turned and ordered everyone to their accommodation and not to leave until further notice. Back at the house, he called the police and sent for the hired hand, who'd gone to find the two men when they failed to show up for work, because he needed to know exactly what had happened. Shortly afterwards, his unsuspecting PA arrived and was instructed to cancel all his appointments for the day, which was annoying because he was due to chair a particularly important county planning meeting

211

that afternoon. The police advance party had already gone into action taping off the scene before Detective Chief Inspector John Roberts arrived, accompanied by his 'bag' man, Detective Sergeant Phil Hammond. After viewing the bodies, the two went straight up to the house to interview Jimmy Edwards and begin establishing the immediate facts while their forensic people got to work. "We have a possible suspect for you, inspector," said Jimmy, inviting them to take a seat at the heavy oak kitchen table. "Well, that would be a most helpful start," he said, introducing his detective sergeant. "It seems we took on a Spanish casual a couple of days ago and now he's disappeared." Who would provide them with the best description? John Roberts asked. "That'll be Corinne, my assistant manager, who will have taken his details and fixed him up in our accommodation. I'll send for her now if you like."

Margo was in the middle of baking when the phone rang. Robin answered it and was shocked to hear Corinne sounding terribly upset. "What on earth's up, my dear?" he asked his voice full of concern. "It's those two new workers I was showing to their cabin the day you and Ben came down. They've been murdered. Someone went to their cabin earlier this morning when they didn't

212

show up for work and found them dead." But perhaps there was some other explanation, like carbon monoxide poisoning, he suggested. "No Robin, they'd both been shot, probably with a silenced gun, and the place is swarming with police and men in white suits and there's even a helicopter flying overhead." She must have thrust her mobile skywards because he thought he just caught the rhythmic sound of beating rotors. "My God. Poor lads," said Robin, who'd now been joined beside the phone by Margo, still holding the heatproof cloth she'd just used to take a tray of homemade savouries out of the oven. "Look you're terribly shaken, so do let me know when you can get away for a couple of hours and I'll come down and pick you up," he said.

"It may not be today because no one's being allowed to leave the farm until they've been interviewed. "Oh, I've got to go; my bleeper's just gone off. It's absolute chaos down here!"

News that there had been some 'serious incident' at the Edwards' farm complex quickly leaked out and Jackie Benson was soon on her way there. It was final copy deadline day so the clock was ticking! Could this possibly have anything to do with the two freed slave labourers she'd driven to the farm to begin their new life

213

a month ago, or was that just too much of a coincidence, she wondered as she approached the farm lane entrance to find her way blocked by a police patrol car, its blue light flashing lazily in the autumn sunshine. "What's going on here, officer?" she asked politely, winding down her window and producing her Press card as he walked over to her. "Can't say, miss, other than that I've been instructed to direct all enquires to our Press Office and to let no one drive up to the farm. She was just tossing up whether to stick around at the scene for a bit or to go back to the office when her mobile sprang into life. It was her colleague, Jock. "Jackie, you'd better get back here as quick as you can. There's been a double murder at the farm and I can't help thinking that the victims may have been those two Polish lads you took under your wing!" Jackie took a moment to take in the terrible news. "Oh no!" she said aloud, ringing off and spinning her car around in the middle of the road under the watchful eye of the police patrol officer. "Bloody media people, always in a hurry!" he muttered.

Jackie sped back into Draymarket, all fizzed up on the adrenalin of having to produce a completely new front page story to replace the one Jock had already ditched.

He and Bill, abandoning all prospects of going off to the Carpenters, were deep in thought as to how to proceed. They'd been alerted to the horrifying facts of the story by a Yardley Upton parish councillor, who'd called them minutes after hearing of the tragedy from a friend who worked at the farm.

By the time Jackie got back and was bounding up the stairs to the office, she'd already decided that her first call was going to be to Margo Lloyd, who'd originally brought the two Polish workers in, because she just might have some more information. Luckily, Robin and Margo had not gone out and before Margo really knew what she was doing, she'd confirmed they'd heard the terrible news from a friend, working at the Edwards farm, that the two murdered men were the ones whose story had been in the paper. "OK" said Jock. "I think that's about all the confirmation we need to splash the story on the double murder at Edwards Farm, saying the dead men are believed to be the two previously held as slave labourers in the old mill cannabis factory and on whose plight this newspaper had previously reported." Bill, now leaning back in his swivel chair, had gone into his customary hands behind head thinking position, "There can't be much doubt that this execution, because that's probably what it was, is linked to the cannabis growing operation over at Little Oreford. That being the case, then why would this gang, whoever they are, go to the trouble of murdering two freed slave labourers, if that's all they were?" Just what was he suggesting Jackie asked. "I'm suggesting we drop any reference to our part in helping this pair, just in case they turn out not to be innocents caught up in a cannabis growing ring, but actually members of this criminal gang who'd had a fall out with their people." He was tempted to add that he'd had a bad feeling about this story from the start, but held his peace.

Not surprisingly, John Roberts, who'd now returned to regional police HQ, was following a similar train of thought and was beginning to question his earlier judgement. He'd interviewed these two after they'd handed themselves in, so had he been too willing to believe their slave worker story in order to remove the case from his bulging in tray? He now strongly suspected that he had. Glancing at his watch, he saw it was 3.45pm. There'd been no time to eat and now he was about to go into the Press Briefing Room to address a vociferous gathering of media people, whose news editors had been badgering the force communication

officer to issue a statement since well before midday
There he confirmed that two farm employees had been
found shot dead in their cabin early that morning,
although they could not be named at that time, and that
an arrest warrant had been issued for a fellow Spanish
worker, who'd since disappeared. He was, however, able
to issue them with a detailed description of the fugitive
and to tell them a photofit image would be released
shortly.

Jackie, having dashed off her Page One lead story,
turned up just as the briefing was coming to an end. She
breathed a sigh of relief on hearing from her colleagues
that the victims had yet to be officially identified and
named. So the Gazette would be getting its scoop, only
without the news that a manhunt had been launched.

Once back in his office, John Roberts and his detective
sergeant were chewing over the fact that no one at the
farm knew anything about the victims, who'd kept
themselves totally to themselves, or had even spoken to
the mystery Spaniard. The fact the two had gone out of
their way to avoid any social contact with their fellow
workers, was in itself suspicious, they concluded. This
was clearly the time to call up the National Crime
Agency drugs people, to whom he'd earlier sent a report

on the Little Oreford mill discovery, because, with a double murder now linked to that case, it was probably a larger and far more dangerous drug production operation than might earlier have been thought.

Corinne called around teatime, saying she could now get away and would indeed be grateful if Robin would come down and pick her up so that she could spend a few hours away from the farm "If you're not needed first thing in the morning, why don't you grab a few overnight things and stay with us?" he suggested. "That would be really nice and actually it's my day off tomorrow, so yes I will, Robin." This wasn't going to be quite the evening they'd planned, he told Margo as, grabbing his car keys from the hall stand, he headed for the door.

Corinne, still looking pretty shaken when she arrived, described how she'd helped the police draw up an identikit picture of the mystery Spaniard, whom she'd interviewed in the farm office and shown to his cabin. "And to think that all along he must have had a gun with a silencer in his backpack and was intent on murdering those two poor young men. "It frightens me just to think about it and how, out of the three spare cabins on the site, I gave him the one next to theirs because, as they were also newcomers, I thought they might get on!"

They all stayed up late and, although Corinne was normally an early riser, she didn't wake until around ten when a shaft of sunlight found its way through a crack in the heavy curtains and fell on her face. Her room overlooked the green and was used by Margo when she wanted to see at a glance what was going on out there. Drawing back the curtains, her attention was caught immediately by a film crew setting up on the grass opposite the mill house with, she assumed, a reporter preparing to do an interview. The media had obviously now found out that the two murdered men were the ones who'd been held as slave labour in the mill. Pulling on the fluffy white dressing gown Margo had said she was most welcome to use, she came barefooted down the stairs just as Robin was coming in through the front door.

"There you are, my dear. You've had a good rest and that's probably just what you needed." He'd been down to the newsagents in Yardley for their weekly copy of the Gazette with its front page banner headline news of the double murder and its link with Little Oreford.

"Just as well our paper is ordered, because all the others were sold out," he told Margo as he entered the kitchen and put their precious copy face up on the kitchen table.

Chapter 23

Tanya Talbot had not seen the paper, but she'd heard the news on her hire car radio as she drove slowly away from the new site, having locked up the house that was now to be left empty until long after all the fuss had died down. She was not in a good mood. The syndicate's decision to dispose of Alek and Danek had been taken because they'd worked at several other locations and had known too much, she'd been told earlier. But from her perspective, it was a stupid move. It would only serve to draw more attention to their operations and had forced the temporary abandoning of the new site after all the work she'd put in to setting it up. Not only that, but because the house was so close to the coast, there had also been the prospect of smuggling more hard drugs in from the continent. What a bloody waste of time and effort it had all been and now it would be quite a while before she could return to an area which, surprisingly, she quite liked. On the other hand, why shouldn't she just risk sticking around for a couple more nights and having a little more fun with her frightened little rabbit, whom she'd come to quite enjoy both sexually teasing and then shocking. Their bondage session, once he'd

220

overcome his innate embarrassment, had really turned her on. He'd been on top, but it was she who'd been in control. 'Perhaps I'll just show up at his house tomorrow night,' she thought. He had already told her quite enough for her to zone in on it from space and even to spot his beloved, newly repaired, sports car sitting on his drive. The look on his face when she'd showed up at the mill in her Merc had been an absolute picture. Yes, the more she thought about it, the more she could feel those feelings slowly rising like a tide inside her. Yes, she would go and pay her little rabbit a surprise visit tomorrow night and she'd take some of her favourite 'toys' with her.

Continuing her drive back to Draymarket, she went over the slightly heated conversation she'd had with Uncle over the killings which had abruptly drawn to a close, when he'd reminded her of the completely unnecessary time she'd suddenly stuck a vegetable chopping knife into another of her little rabbits because he'd displeased her.

Tanya popped in to Hendon Motors and arranged to drop off her hire car keys and pick up her Merc just before they closed on the Sunday afternoon. She now had the rest of the day to pack and go through her tediously familiar, fingerprint removing exercise, before paying one last visit to Royston, after which she'd be long gone.

That particular Sunday was not to be a day of rest for John Roberts and his colleague, who now had a nasty double murder on their patch. The surprise premature release of the victims' identities by the media before the time of his choosing was now becoming a source of acute embarrassment to him. Others higher up his chain of command had also come to the conclusion that maybe the two 'slave labourers' he'd released from custody, were not as innocent as they'd claimed to have been.

Maybe if they'd been held longer and put under more pressure, then this story might have had an entirely different outcome with lives being saved! "No point in beating ourselves up over this," he said to Phil Hammond. "The Spanish hit man will be long gone, but if the NCA has a picture list of suspects thought to be involved in cannabis farming and other drug-related operations, then we could show it to those people we know came into contact with them, just in case anything was thrown up. I know It's a long shot, but at this stage anything's worth a try."

222

Royston was up early that Sunday morning because Alicia was coming to supper and he wanted to have a proper tidy up before driving over to the Allway Centre to stock up with provisions for the special candlelit supper he was going to prepare for her. Robin and Margo and Ben and Laura had slipped into the routine of taking it in turn to host a Sunday family brunch. On this particular day, it was to be held in the cottage with Corinne as an extra guest because she'd decided to take the whole weekend off and was still with them.

All was in full swing when the phone rang and Robin walked into the study to answer it, glancing down at the scattering of plans for the Broadway Villas alterations on his desk as he did so. Two minutes later he was back in the kitchen. "Ben, that was the police asking if you and I could pop into the Regional Police HQ to look at pictures of suspects thought to be involved with cannabis growing operations and other drug related crimes, just in case we might have seen any of them around here. I knew you'd be at work tomorrow so I provisionally said we'd go over this afternoon. I'll drive because I'd like to pop into Hendon Motors on the way back and see what they've got by way of used cars as mine's overdue a change."

Ben and Laura, who'd become used to Robin occasionally making assumptions on their behalf, exchanged glances and agreed it would be OK by them. Margo also thought it would be fine. "We three girls could all spend some quality time together and maybe take Luke and Lottie over to their favourite play barn complex," she said, looking at Laura, who again felt slightly annoyed at being organised. Just for a moment she was tempted to say she'd planned to take the kids swimming, but then the prospect of visiting the play barn had met with their instant approval, so she thought better of it.

There were literally hundreds of small portrait sized images for Robin and Ben to flick through. They'd been provided with a couple of paper cups of coffee and were twenty minutes into the task with their eyes beginning to strain, when Robin suddenly leaned forward and pointed to the slightly blurred picture of a young woman on the far right of a row towards the bottom of the screen. With a couple of clicks he'd brought the single image to full size and was staring intently at it. "I've seen her recently, I know I have, but where?" Ben studied the woman intently. "She's quite a stunner, which is why she might have stood out in a crowd, but that could have been anywhere," he suggested. "No, I don't think so because it's somehow more positive than that."

They'd finished the trawl a couple of minutes later and having pointed out the possible suspect image to Detective Sergeant Hammond, were on their way to Hendon's in Draymarket.

"This is so annoying. It's like when someone's name is on the tip of your tongue and you can't quite get it," said Robin, who was still grinding through the gears of his memory as he pulled into Hendon's and started looking for somewhere to park, as the forecourt was being repaved. They eventually found a space along one of the gleaming lines of price tagged cars behind the showroom and were weaving their way on a more direct route through the vehicles towards the slick looking reception area when Robin suddenly stopped in his tracks. Now almost in front of him was a blue Mercedes sports coupe! "My God, it's hers!" Ben followed his friend's gaze. "Whose, Robin?" Ben asked. "The woman in the picture. She turned up with Royston Randall when I went to view the Old Mill House. She was holding his clipboard and I assumed she was his assistant. He introduced her as an 'interested party,' but I think from something Laura said later, she might have been a

225

friend. You remember, she told us that, a young and expensively dressed woman had come into Randall's one evening, just before closing time, asking for Royston. When told he was expected back from a viewing shortly, had then said she'd wait for him over at the pub. Now we'd better find out from the sales team, who she is and what her car's doing here."

A quick scan of the showroom revealed three suited salesman all at their desks and deep in conversation with customers and close by, a seating area with several others waiting.

"This won't do," muttered Robin, advancing on the nearest desk and interrupting the conversation. The surprised looks on the middle-aged salesman's face and those of his customers, showed they were not best pleased, but Robin brushed that aside, asking for the manager or the proprietor on a matter of great urgency.

"He's busy in the office, so if you gentleman will both kindly take a seat, I'll find out if he will see you when I have finished talking to my customers." That would not do because they needed to see the manager right away, he retorted.

Seeing Robin was not taking 'no' for an answer, the salesman rose from behind his desk, apologising to the couple he was serving as he did so, and led them across the showroom to a door half-hidden behind a screen in the corner. He knocked and put his head inside. "John, I have a couple of gents out here insisting on seeing you," he said, placing a heavy emphasis on the word 'insisting'. "Better show them in then." The voice was measured with a note of authority, which Robin recognised immediately from his long years in the Civil Service and automatically adjusted his approach to match it. "John Hendon. How can I help you gentlemen?" he asked, inviting them to take a seat in front of his large, paper strewn desk. They'd hardly done so and were just beginning to explain the reason for their intrusion when a muted, but still deep throated roar drifted in through an open window and was instantly recognised by Robin from that fateful Monday morning after his viewing of the old mill. "That sounds like the Merc coupe," he said. "Certainly is," agreed John Hendon. They all turned to the large picture window just in time to see the coupe pull out onto the road and vanish from sight.

Chapter 24

Alicia Wiltshire had been playing tennis all afternoon at the Yardley Upton Club, which she'd joined soon after moving to the area, and was now enjoying a long hot soak in the bath and looking forward to her evening with Royston.

He'd arranged to pick her up around seven and take her back with him because there was very little spare parking at his place. She was staying over and her small overnight bag was lying open on her bed waiting a final packing.

Her relationship with Royston was developing well. He was a nice, thoughtful chap and it was really good to have someone to spend some of her free time with again, but whether she'd actually wanted to make it a permanent arrangement at some point, she was not altogether sure. Then there was Peter. She'd told him she was now seeing someone in order to dissuade him from moving to Bristol, but it seemed to have had the opposite effect. Oh dear. He'd started texting her nearly every day and now she'd started ignoring his messages.

Alicia was all packed and hovering by the front door, when Royston arrived a little ahead of time and they decided it would be nice to start the evening with a quick one at The Lion before going back to his place.

When Robin and Ben had finished explaining the situation to John, he handed them the phone to call Detective Chief Inspector Roberts on his direct line because, luckily Robin still had his card in his wallet. The chief inspector's line quickly switched to answer phone inviting a message or a call to his mobile. Frustratingly, Robin was not quick enough to take the number down on the pad, thrust across the desk at him, so had to repeat the process all over again, only to receive another leave a message or call the station instruction. This time he was able to take down the number and make the call through to a switchboard where he asked to speak to the most senior officer available, as a matter of urgency, and was put through to Police Control.

The duty sergeant, he was told, was on his break, so if he'd leave his number someone would call him back.

Now there was nothing to do other than to thank John Hendon for his help and go home.

Robin was expecting the call all the way back to Little Oreford, but it never came. The sergeant had returned from his break and had been given the message, but didn't have time to deal with it, because he and his colleagues suddenly became totally involved with a fatal major pile-up on the North Devon link road involving at least two lorries and a number of cars.

"Good evening, Mr Randall. You've just missed The Demons, haven't they, Pet?" said Landlord Geoff Hodges, turning to his wife. They ordered a bottle of good red wine with a screw top to start now and take with them, while Royston explained to Alicia that his colleagues, Hannah and Heather, had a fearsome reputation as the two not to play against on pub quiz nights. "They're so good, they're not allowed to play together anymore and the teams they do play for invariably end up winning."

Most of the bar tables were already occupied so they ended up perching on the end of a long one where a family were half way through their meal. Then Royston was spotted by the village window cleaner, who wandered over, pint in hand, for a chat, attracted, moth to candle, by Alicia. He'd observed her several times working in her classroom after school and certainly liked what he saw. The result was that they stayed in The Lion far longer than intended, while Johnny Windows, as he liked to be known, went on at some length about the murders at Edwards Farm.

"That's one of the small disadvantages of friendly village life, in that it can become a little too friendly at times," said Royston as they drove slowly home, passing the spot where he'd had his nasty accident. For one fleeting moment he thought of telling her how it had catapulted Tanya into his life, but then thought better of it. He'd left the side lamps on in his comfortable lounge, because he knew they'd be casting a cosy welcoming glow by the time they returned. Alicia settled herself in one of his two big armchairs with another glass of the red wine and casually flicked through one of the glossy classic car magazines on the coffee table while Royston busied himself in the kitchen. The table was all set in the dining area and Royston was just lifting the salmon fillets out of the oven when the doorbell rang. "Shall I answer it darling?" Alicia asked, rising from her chair. She'd only recently started using the endearment and Royston liked that. It was just another small sign of their quietly growing intimacy. "If you would, please, but I don't know who it could possibly be, because I'm certainly not expecting anyone."

Alicia made her way into the hall and opened the front door.

"Oh, I wasn't expecting Royston to have company!" There was a slight note of annoyance in the voice of the strikingly attractive blonde younger woman, standing there in front of her, wine bottle in hand. "Well, aren't you going to invite me in?" she asked. "No, I'm not sure that I am," replied Alicia, who was taller than this rude interloper and certainly no pushover when it came to being confronted.

"Royston, I think you'd better come here, darling." Now she was using the endearment to assert her authority over this unexpected challenger. "Oh, darling, is it now?" Tanya retorted, suddenly pushing past Alicia and walking along the short hallway into the lounge. "Well, this is all very cosy and domestic I must say," she said glancing around the room and then straight at Royston, who'd emerged from the kitchen still wearing his cooking apron. "Tanya, what on earth are you doing here?" he demanded feeling an anger at having his home so suddenly and shockingly invaded. "Well, I could ask you what's she's doing here," she countered, nodding at Alicia now standing far more uncertainly in the doorway. "That's the trouble with men. Most will be two-timers, given half a chance," she said turning slightly and addressing herself to Alicia. "Look Tanya, I suggest you turn around and leave right now," demanded Royston, feeling an outraged anger welling up inside him. "And if I choose not to what are you going to do about it?" she asked. "Then I'll call the police," threatened Royston reaching for the mobile he'd just happened to have left on his sideboard.

"Oh yes. You go ahead and call the police, who'll certainly not appreciate being drawn into a domestic between a respected local estate agent and the two women he'd been cheating on?

Think what the Gazette would make of that if I was arrested and had to appear in the local magistrates' court, where I would reveal all. Make no mistake about that. No, I'm not going to go so you might as well pour me a glass of that wine, darling."

Alicia who'd been silently watching from the side line, suddenly stepped forward and grabbed the phone.

"We're calling the police, so you might as well leave before this does turn into a domestic, as you put it," she said, looking at Royston for support. "Oh well, have it your own way," replied Tanya, slowly putting her unopened bottle down on the edge of the dining table, all neatly set for a cosy dinner for two. Reaching into her expensive Italian leather shoulder bag, she pulled out a small hand gun. "There's already been one double murder in this neighbourhood, so let's hope there's not going to be another!"

When Robin and Ben got back to the cottage, Margo wasn't there because she'd volunteered to take Corinne back to the farm and Laura had gone home with the children.

"I've got a very nasty feeling about all this," said Robin, disappearing into his study and calling the police once more, only to be told that the control room team were now heavily involved in a major incident and that his inquiry would just have to wait until the morning.

When Ben got home, he told Laura what had happened and that Robin was sure the image he'd spotted in the police file of wanted persons was indeed the woman who'd been with Royston Randall on the morning he'd viewed the old mill house. "And just to think that while we were in John Hendon's office, she drove off in her coupe, while we could only watch from the window," he said. "From how you've described her in the picture, I think she must be the woman, who came into our office looking for Royston that afternoon, but according to

Hannah and Heather, he's now in a budding relationship with our tenant." Margo returned home to the cottage shortly after Ben had left. She and Robin watched a game show, had a first cursory glance through the Sunday papers, which would last them all week, and an early supper, but he couldn't settle to anything.

"It's no good," he said, half to himself and half to Margo. "Royston Randall needs to be warned he's been involved with a woman on a most wanted list and I'm not going to leave it until the morning!" Margo thought her brother was perhaps overreacting a little. So, what was he going to do? she asked. "Laura works in the estate agency and will probably know where her boss lives so I'll go over and ask," said Robin, grabbing his jacket and hurrying back across the green to Albany House.

"Stupid as it may seem, I don't know, other than it's out in the country, somewhere towards Yardley," admitted Laura as they stood together in the hallway. "But I'll bet our tenant will know, if she is romantically involved with Royston, so why don't I just call her and ask?" she said, walking through to the kitchen and using the wall mounted phone, but getting no reply.

"What's up, Robin?" asked Ben, who was sitting at the table when they'd both walked in. "I'm worried Royston could be in some danger from this woman and I don't want to wait until tomorrow before warning him." He could see that his friend was being deadly serious.

"Well, Laura, surely your office colleagues, Hannah and Heather, will have the answer," suggested Ben.

Laura agreed they'd be bound to know, but stupidly she didn't have their home number and only knew they lived in the barn conversion close to the pub. "I'll bet someone in The Lion will know exactly where they live, so why don't we drive down there now and ask?" suggested Ben, who was beginning to think Robin was right about not leaving things until the morning.

"Christ, Tanya. Put that thing away." Royston felt his throat going suddenly dry as his anger dissolved into pure fear. He knew, from all his past knowledge of her, that she was compulsive and totally unpredictable and he had no doubt that she could, if she wanted, murder them both there and then. In a flash his mind went back to The old mill house and her interest in looking around the building and then he thought of those poor lads, who'd worked there and had been slaughtered as they slept!

Alicia, unaware of all this, could only see that Royston had somehow become entangled with this deranged woman, who was now pointing a gun at them and then she was thinking about the double murder which had been all over the media.

"No point in letting that lovely meal go to waste, my little rabbit, so why don't you go into the kitchen and share it out for three, while your other girlfriend and I make ourselves comfortable at the table," she said.

Tanya, with the small gun in one hand, walked casually across the room and dragged a third chair to the table placing herself in the middle with her now perhaps intended victims at either end, because she'd yet to make up her mind what she was going to do. "Did you know he just loves bondage sex since I introduced him to it?" Alicia, now completely terrified, said she'd not really known Royston long enough for that. "So when did you come onto the scene and how do you know my little rabbit then?" Royston, now listening to the conversation as he went numbly through the motions of serving up the meal, looked wildly around for some means of resistance His eyes came to rest on a small sharp knife thrusting itself handle first out of its wooden resting block. Could he conceal it in his back pocket or under the heat-proof cloth he'd be holding to bring the oven hot dishes into the living room? The very thought of doing so, scared him.

One sign of resistance and he knew she'd shoot them both there and then. It was only a couple of steps to the door into the garden and the key was in the lock. Could he open it without her hearing so at least they might have at least one means of escape? But the key was sometimes difficult to turn; he'd meant to fix it a dozen times, but never got around to it.

Heart thumping, he advanced on the key, grabbing a tea towel which might muffle the sound of the mechanism, but no, the wretched key refused to budge. Snatches of conversation reaching him from the lounge, told him she'd not been alerted, so he gave it another desperate twist and it finally turned.

Should he escape and raise the alarm? No, he couldn't leave Alicia alone with this crazy woman and he also knew it was not the time for knife hiding heroics. They'd just have to go along with her and hope she was just playing a game with them and that the gun was an imitation, although he knew it his heart that it probably wasn't.

Returning to the lounge, he placed the salmon with its garnish of fresh vegetables in front of them and walked

238

back into the kitchen for his own. "Before you sit down, Royston dear, be a love, bring me a glass and open my wine. It's a good white and will go far better with the fish than the red plonk you're drinking." Alicia sat frozen in her seat as she watched Royston going through the motions of doing as he was bid. This mad woman had now placed her small gun down just out of reach on her side of the table, but surely, Alicia thought, she could easily make a grab for it if Tanya happened to get distracted for a moment or if she should just happen to pick up her knife and fork together. The thought of having a plan somehow calmed her just a little, but it was not to be, because once Royston had poured Tanya her wine, she suddenly rose from the table, taking up the gun as she did so. "I've gone off food, so I'll just sit on the sofa and allow you two love birds to enjoy your meal."

Ben drove as fast as he dared down through the lanes to Hampton Green. They'd decided to go first to Cherry Grove, just in case Alicia had not heard the phone, but the house was in darkness and her small car was on the drive. "She must be away for the weekend," said Ben, swinging around at the end of the small cul-de-sac and heading for The Lion. It was now around 9pm and the early evening diners and drinkers had melted away leaving Landlord Geoff and his wife, Pet, to begin their customary Sunday evening tidy-up.

They'd not be opening again until the following evening when their relief team would be in, so they'd be having a welcome day off. Geoff, who was now feeling just a little demob happy, recognised Ben and Robin as soon as they came in. "What can I get you, gents?" he asked. "Sadly, we're not after a drink," said Robin. "What come into my pub, but not to have a drink? No wonder rural pubs are closing down all over the country." He gave them a wink. "Don't take any notice of him, so how can we help you?" said Pet, coming to the rescue. She hadn't spotted the wink. "We're trying to get in touch with Royston Randall, your village estate agent, on a matter of some urgency, so we were wondering if you just happened to know where he lives," explained Robin. "Oh, he was in here earlier with that new teacher from the school, but we don't know where he lives, do we, Geoff?" The landlord agreed, but said The Demons would definitely know. "Who are The Demons?" asked Ben. "They're his assistants and they live in the barn conversion at the end of the lane next to the church."

A few minutes later, they were pulling into the wide drive, in front of the barn. There were two cars parked there and thankfully the lights in the house were on. Heather instantly recognised Robin as the purchaser of Albany House and invited them in to the huge oak beamed living room. "Han, we have visitors," she called. Of course, they knew where Royston lived, but what was all this about?

"I'm sorry, but there's no time for explanation," said Robin heading for the front door.

"This can't really be happening," thought Royston as he sat looking at a deathly pale Alicia at the other end of the table. Neither had any stomach for the food which they were both pushing around their plates, taking the occasional mouthful. "Don't bother to clear up Royston. Let's see what's on telly," said Tanya, now bored of watching them sitting at the table in terrified silence. Waving them to the sofa, she told Royston to use the remote lying on a side table before curling herself into the large single armchair almost opposite them. "You choose, darling, because I don't mind what I watch. but maybe one of those stand-up comedy shows would be good." Royston began flicking through the channels until he found a comedy chat show.

"Look Tanya, I don't know quite what I've done to upset you, but surely this has all gone quite far enough." The look she gave him was terrifying. "Not know what you've done to upset me. Two-timed me with this particularly unattractive woman. That's what you've done. I feel insulted.

"Did you know Royston was seeing me?" she demanded, turning her now demented gaze on Alicia, who could only shake her head in response. "No, of course you didn't. That's the trouble with men, they're all horny rats. who'll all cheat, given half a chance." Then Royston tried reasoning with her. "You've realised, she didn't know about us and is a completely innocent party, so why don't you allow her to leave?" he begged. "What and call the police? I don't think so, but I've got a better idea.

"This programme is crap, so why don't you two love birds start undressing each other and have a fuck on the sofa? Now that would be far more entertaining." Alicia stole a frightened glance at Royston and started to crying. She couldn't take any more. "Waterworks won't help," said Tanya, taking up the pistol, she'd left on the arm of the chair and waving it at them.

Ben and Robin drove in silence back through a series of winding lanes towards Yardley Upton, going as fast as they dared. Heather had given them Boss's post code, which was certainly a help, otherwise the chances were that they'd take a wrong turning. It was now clear that Alicia Wiltshire was spending the evening with Royston, but when they'd reached the chequered flag on Ben's satnav, there was the Mercedes on the drive just inside the gates!

"What the hell do you suppose is going on in there?" said Robin, pulling in to the layby opposite, switching off his engine and reducing his voice to a whisper. Had the Merc not been in the drive, they'd have knocked on Royston's front door and delivered their warning, but this was now an entirely different situation. "We can hardly go in and warn him about Tanya when she's also in the room, now can we?" said Robin. "You may have made a mistake and she could well be totally innocent," suggested Ben. "I don't think so. I'm going to call 999 and to hang with the consequences," Robin replied. "Look before you do, I'll sneak around the side of the house just in case I can see in through a window and that will probably tell us what's going on if anything." Before Robin could stop him, Ben had slipped out of the car and was moving cat-like up the drive and off into the garden.

'What the hell am I doing,' he asked himself as he moved silently past an illuminated frieze glass side door, which probably led into the kitchen, and towards a large picture window now displaying a shaft of light through a crack in the curtains just large enough for him to peep through. What he saw that night would be seared on his memory forever. Royston Randall and Alicia Wiltshire were standing naked in front of one another, various items of clothing scattered at their feet, and, there just off to the right, sat Tanya Talbot, a small gun in her hand. "Oh my God," Ben muttered as he fled the scene and was quickly back in the car. "Dial 999 now, Robin. Tanya's in the living room. She's clearly ordered Royston and Alicia to undress and she's sitting watching them with a gun in her hand."

Minutes later, having made the call, Ben and Robin sat there in confusion, not knowing what to do next. "It's going to take at least thirty minutes for them to arrive by which time she could have murdered both of them," said Ben. "There's a side door and I'll see if it's open and, if by any chance it is, you could go and bang on the front door while I sneak in through there."

244

In that moment, Robin was remembering his friend disappearing over the mill wall with Laura yelling at him to stop.

"Ben, we must wait for the police because any sudden disturbance might frighten her into pulling the trigger and then we'd be blamed for taking the law into our own hands with disastrous consequences." Ben hesitated. "Yes, but what might she do when she hears the police sirens because they're bound to be on?"

Before Robin could object any further, Ben had gone again and was back a couple of minutes later, saying the side door was indeed open. "Right. That'll be very useful for the police to know when they get here," said Robin, who'd made up his mind they'd be crazy to try to intervene and was already back on the phone to the police, praying it would not be too late to silence their sirens.

Back inside the bungalow, Royston and Alicia had undressed and were standing there naked in front of one another, frozen to the spot. "Well, get on with it then, darling, do your stuff!"

Alicia's face was wet with tears and in that moment, Royston knew he could go no further and started nodding his head in silent defiance. The gun exploded with a roar, the bullet smashing into a large racing car picture on the far side of the room, its glass shattering and crashing to the floor. "Get on with it, I said." Royston shaken out of his defiance reached out and put his arms around Alicia's waist. "That's better, darling. Now start kissing," she demanded.

With the sound of the gun going off, Ben and Robin were out of the car in an instant. There was now no question of waiting for the police. Moments later Robin was pounding on the front door while Ben was already in the kitchen and peering cautiously around the door into the living room, where Royston and Alicia were now sprawling on the sofa. "What an inconvenient time to have visitors. I think we'll just ignore them because they're sure to give up and go away," said Tanya. But the banging continued.

Looking half sideways with Royston now on top of her, Alicia had a fleeting vision of Ben as he tore across the room, snatched up the half empty wine bottle from the table and smashed Tanya over the head with all the force he could muster.

She crumpled to the floor, dropping the gun as she did so and lay motionless, the back of her head now a mess of blood and red wine. "Thank God!" uttered Royston, getting to his feet, grabbing the gun from where it lay close to Tanya's outstretched hand, and turning to comfort Alicia, who had broken into an uncontrollable flood of tears. "You two get dressed while I go and let my friend in and call for an ambulance," said Ben, now hearing the faint sound of a wailing siren. Twenty minutes later, Tanya Talbot, was being hurriedly attended by two medics, who finding her still alive, but unconscious, rushed her off to Ben's hospital. All Alicia wanted to do was to go home and if she never saw Royston Randall again, she'd be happy, but it was several hours before they were all released and Robin and Ben drove her back to Cherry Grove. "Are you sure you wouldn't prefer to come home with me because my sister, Margo, would only be too pleased if you did," said Robin. But Alicia assured them she'd be all right, because she'd already decided she was going to run a warm bath and have a long soak to cleanse herself of her terrible ordeal.

The full story, when it came out in all its horrendous and embarrassing details, made the national news and easily convinced Alicia that she no longer wished to live or work in Hampton Green. The school governors agreed that, in view of all the circumstances, she could leave at the end of the autumn term. Royston made several attempts to see her and to explain his side of the story, but without success and was soon seeking a new tenant for the house in Cherry Grove.

Alicia moved in with a tennis club girlfriend in Draymarket where she received a long letter from Royston, addressed to the school and delivered the day before she was due to leave. It set out in detail all the circumstances leading up to their horrific ordeal and it came to her that had she committed herself to him on the night of their supper at hers instead of going off to spend the weekend with Peter, then he probably would not have been tempted to see Tanya again and they might have been spared their terrible ordeal.

As the weeks went by Alicia, whose confidence had been severely shaken, began realising she was missing Royston and that when she was in a better place, she would see him again, if that was what he still wanted.

Royston sold his bungalow because it was too painful to go on living there and moved into Draymarket, to be at the centre of his expanding estate agency business.

Tanya Talbot was attended in a private room and held under police guard until she was well enough to be moved on remand to a woman's prison. She was later sent for trial, but her case never resulted in a full hearing with pleas, because when the extent of her past psychopathic activities came to light, she was found to be bordering on the criminally insane and transferred to a secure psychiatric hospital from where she was never likely to return. The National Crime Agency drugs team, realising after the double killing, that the old mill cannabis operation was part of a far larger criminal enterprise, were given a couple of lucky breaks when investigating the affairs of Theresa Thompson, alias Tanya Talbot, via her laptop and mobile phone and after a relatively short investigation, were finally able to close down the whole nationwide operation.

Robin and Margo read all about it in the Sunday papers, but really had their minds on other more important matters because it looked as if their plans to reopen the coaching inn were going to be approved and then they could move on to their far more ambitious old mill house project.

Encouraged by Ben, Laura Jameson and Corinne Potter took blood tests for the record which proved beyond doubt, that they were twins. Corinne wanted to go on and try to discover what had become of their mum, Charlie, but Laura had changed her mind. Sometimes it was better to leave the past undisturbed because who could tell what else might come to light and she'd already had enough surprises to last her a lifetime. Corinne said that was OK by her, she and Robin now being completely wrapped up in plans for reopening the inn.

Much to his surprise, Ben accepted he was a man of action if desperate circumstance justified it, but he wouldn't have been human if he hadn't started suffering flashbacks from that spur of the moment when he smashed Tanya over the head with the wine bottle. He was offered and accepted some counselling and the help of hospital management colleagues, who were more than generous with the time off they allowed him after the incident. By and by he came to see that, in reality, he'd taken the only action open to him.

Luke and Lottie were upset when Miss Wiltshire left their school, but soon forgot about her and were looking forward to Christmas when their mum would at last realise her dream of decorating the lovely old wooden staircase at Albany House.

THE END

NEXT: Read Albany House – Part Two: The Homecoming.

Printed in Great Britain
by Amazon

17974699R00142